Annan Water

Also by Kate Thompson:

The Switchers Trilogy
Switchers
Midnight's Choice
Wild Blood
(Now available in one volume)

The Missing Link Trilogy
The Missing Link
Only Human
Origins

The Beguilers
(winner of the Irish Bisto Award 2002)
The Alchemist's Apprentice
(winner of the Irish Bisto Award 2003)

Annan Water

KATE THOMPSON

THE BODLEY HEAD
London

ANNAN WATER
A BODLEY HEAD BOOK 0 370 32822 1

Published in Great Britain by The Bodley Head,
an imprint of Random House Children's Books

This edition published 2004

1 3 5 7 9 10 8 6 4 2

Papers used by Random House Children's Books are natural, recyclable
products made from wood grown in sustainable forests. The
manufacturing processes conform to the environmental regulations
of the country of origin.

Set in 13.5/16.5 Garamond by
Falcon Oast Graphic Art Ltd

RANDOM HOUSE CHILDREN'S BOOKS
61–63 Uxbridge Road, London W5 5SA
A division of The Random House Group Ltd
RANDOM HOUSE AUSTRALIA (PTY) LTD
20 Alfred Street, Milsons Point, Sydney,
New South Wales 2061, Australia
RANDOM HOUSE NEW ZEALAND LTD
18 Poland Road, Glenfield, Auckland 10, New Zealand
RANDOM HOUSE (PTY) LTD
Endulini, 5A Jubilee Road, Parktown 2193, South Africa

THE RANDOM HOUSE GROUP Limited Reg. No. 954009
www.kidsatrandomhouse.co.uk

A CIP catalogue record for this book is available from the British
Library.

Printed and bound in Great Britain by
Mackays of Chatham plc, Chatham, Kent

For Isobelle

'Annan Waters'

Versions of this song, some under the title 'Allan Water',
date back as far as the late seventeenth century. It was
collected by Francis James Child in the 1890s and published
in volume 4 of *The English and Scottish Popular Ballads*.
I first heard it sung by Phil Callery in Kinvara a few years
ago. He has recorded it, as 'Annan Waters', on his CD *From
the Edge of Memory*, which was released in 1999. It is his
version of the song that is used in the book.

Kate Thompson, 2004

Michael was in no doubt that the mare would jump the gate. Even though he had turned her head away from it, he could tell that she was still thinking about it. She fretted and snatched at the bit, her hocks under her, her front feet barely making contact with the wet ground. Beside her the big chestnut cob stood like a rock, wasting no energy. Michael tugged at his bridle, trying to wake him up and prepare him for what he was required to do.

The mare plunged forward, wrenching Michael's shoulder and almost tearing the cob's reins out of his hand. He pulled her up. She was getting into a stew, defeating the whole purpose of the exercise. He slackened the reins and spoke softly. The mare relaxed, but her ears still twitched. She hadn't forgotten the gate.

Michael hadn't either. He looked back at it.

There was no way of opening it without the right tools. Wire had been wrapped around the posts at both ends and stapled to the wood. It no longer functioned as a gate, but as part of a boundary, separating the land his parents were renting from the next farm. But there had been a time, not all that long ago perhaps, when the green lane he could see on the other side of it had been a thoroughfare. It was overgrown now with low branches and reaching brambles, and it was impossible for Michael to see how far it went before it petered out, or met a metalled road. He wanted to find out.

'Take her out for a hack today,' Jean had said. 'Sweeten her up a bit.'

After yesterday. For two hours he had ridden her in the jumps paddock beneath his mother's expert eye. Circling and circling and circling; winding the mare down, trying to get her steady and concentrated. Every time she came within reach of a fence she gathered herself, her head went up, she began to track sideways. And every time, Jean had said the same thing.

'Circle her again. Nice and tight. Outside leg.'

The mare was brilliant; a jumping genius. She never stopped, and never touched a pole unless it was the rider's fault. But she was giddy as a gadfly; perpetually on the boil. She was already a Grade A jumping pony when they bought her, but she was cheap all the same. She had changed hands some time before, and her new rider had been too inexperienced to handle a pony with her temperament. She had been over-jumped and under-schooled. When Jean and Frank bought her six months ago, she was completely unmanageable. It was Michael's job to sort her out.

She was getting there. In a few days' time they would be taking her to a show for the first time since they got her. That was why they had worked her so intensively the day before. That was why Jean had sent her out with Michael for a quiet hack.

'You can take Bandit with you,' she had said. 'If he doesn't steady her, nothing will.'

Michael looked at him, standing patiently beside the fidgeting mare, resting a hind leg. If ever a horse was misnamed, it was him. There was no more gentle-manly horse in the yard. From time to time Michael rode him in the Grade D and E classes at the shows. He jumped perfectly every time; never put a foot wrong. But his size was against him. He was a heavy cob, not far from a draught horse, and he didn't have the speed and agility that was needed to win a jump-off. Out hunting he was like a tank; anything he couldn't get over, he went through. He would have made a brilliant horse for a keen amateur rider, but his type was out of fashion. He'd been in the string for a year, and despite their best efforts they couldn't find a buyer for him.

Michael wouldn't have considered jumping the gate

leading any other horse. It was a seriously risky under-taking. But Bandit had brains and he used them. If any horse would do it, he would. Michael glanced back at it again. If they didn't go over the gate, he would have to go back to the yard and hack out along the main road. It was the one thing his parents hadn't taken into account when they rented the farm at the beginning of the year. In Yorkshire, where they had lived before, there was a maze of small country lanes around their yard, ideal for riding out. But although there were small roads here, there was no way of getting to them without going a good distance along the trunk road.

It didn't seem to bother Jean and Frank. Horses had broken most of the bones in their bodies. Horses had broken their hearts as well, when their youngest daughter had been dragged to her death by a bolting pony. Only their nerves remained intact. They both seemed immune to danger. Michael had never seen either of them afraid of any horse in the yard, and there had been some pretty bad ones, even within his memory. When it came to the roads, their attitudes corresponded to their general philosophy. If a horse was afraid of traffic, what better way to cure him than to take him into the thick of it?

Michael didn't share their views. Hunting or jumping, he was as courageous as either of them, but he'd had some close calls out exercising on the roads, and he saw no sense in looking for trouble. That was why he was there, measuring up the gate yet again; longing to explore the peaceful lane beyond it.

He made up his mind; backtracked a short distance, tightened his girth, gave Bandit a few digs with his toe in the hope of waking him up. It made no perceptible difference, but the pony picked up on the tension and was already bouncing on the spot when Michael turned her. She reared and leaped forward into a bucketing canter. There was a momentary resistance from the cob, and then he was alongside. Two strides before the jump, Michael sat deep into the saddle and pushed the mare on. She stood way off the gate; took a great lion's leap at it; cleared it by yards. The gelding was in the air beside her, taking the five bars in his usual, economical style.

They were over.

The green track stretched away ahead of them, and the little mare reached for it like a thoroughbred on the gallops. Michael wrestled with her and, when all else failed, turned her head into the hedgerow. She fought him, trying to keep racing on crabwise, but she couldn't keep it up. She had to stop.

It wasn't until then that a tide of emotions, entirely unexpected, rolled in upon Michael. There was relief, at having got over the gate so easily, but even stronger than that was a sense of elation, as though that jump had freed him from a lot more than the traffic on the A72. There had been something illicit – illegal even – about the decision; the leap; the secrecy of it all. Between these high hedges he was invisible; a free and independent spirit in a world of his own, new and unexplored.

He praised the mare and tugged at her ear. He flattered the cob as well, liking him suddenly; sorry for him because his plain looks concealed such an honest and generous heart.

It was clear that the track hadn't been used for years. Beyond the first bend it narrowed even further. Ash and hawthorn reached in from either side and made an irregular arch, beneath which Michael had to duck from time to time. At the most overgrown parts, even the horses had to drop their heads and push through, ears first. Brambles and blackthorn snagged Michael's jacket and leggings. He had to keep his arm up to shield his face, and could hardly see where he was going. But the mare seemed to be as thrilled by the adventure as he was and pushed impetuously on. Bandit fell in behind her, taking the slaps from the whipping-back branches with no complaint beyond the occasional long-suffering sigh.

Michael was afraid that the path would end too soon, and his freedom along with it. For a stretch it became even more choked, with tall, dark weeds underfoot and every kind of thorny shrub competing for the scant light. Then, without warning, the way ahead was clear. There was a gateway into a field on the right-hand side, and tractor tyres had formed deep ruts right up to it from the other, unknown end of the track. Scraps of black silage wrapping clung to the roughly trimmed hedges. A few muddy cattle stood in a corner of the field and watched the horses with mild curiosity.

Between the tyre tracks, the grass was short and the ground was firm. The mare was already skittering sideways, itching to get up some speed. Michael shortened his reins and let her canter on, but cautiously; steadily. The cob fell in alongside, foot perfect despite being half in and half out of the muddy ruts.

The lane swung this way and that, almost animate in its twisting and turning and tempting. Through gaps in the bushes, Michael could see farmland on either side, tired grassland mostly, waiting for the spring. There were sheep with new lambs in one of the meadows. They scattered in surprise, making the mare shy, then bleated after them reproachfully.

The grassy lane invited them on. The pony would have lobbed along for ever, enjoying the novelty, if Michael hadn't noticed that she was breaking into a sweat and remembered that she was supposed to be having an easy day. He pulled her up.

She was reluctant to stop, but as soon as she did, she relaxed, as though she had let off her surplus steam and was grateful for the rare opportunity to walk. Michael kicked his feet out of their stirrups and let his long legs dangle. His feet almost reached the mare's knees. It embarrassed him that he was so tall, but still not out of ponies yet.

The track wandered on between the fields. Michael found a contentment he hadn't known for years, and as though to confirm him in it, the sun found a gap in the clouds and spilled through, marbling the ground with the shadows of the bare branches. After another half a mile or so they came to a narrow, tarmacked road, but even that wasn't the end of the path. On the opposite side it ran on again and, as though the pony was as curious about it as her rider, she looked neither right nor left along the road but crossed straight over.

More hedges, more gates, more twists and turns. The sun went in again and a few drops of rain splashed off Michael's oilskin. It didn't matter. He had learned not to care about rain. His parents rarely took account of the weather. Like traffic, it was one of the irritations of the business, not to be allowed to interfere with routine.

'If God had intended us to stay out of the rain, why did He make us waterproof?'

Michael had heard Frank say it far too often. Even thinking about it threatened to put him in a foul mood. He looked at his watch. He had already been out for more than an hour, and it would take him as long to get back. He must have covered three or four miles already.

He decided to give it another fifteen minutes, but it didn't take that long. As they rounded a long, sweeping curve Michael saw the wet grey gleam of another metalled road, bordered on its far side by a stone wall. When they reached it, the mare hesitated, as though bewildered by the sudden return to the present day. She didn't stop, though, but turned to her right and set out purposefully, her feet clacking on the tarmac.

Michael tried to turn her back, but she resisted, drawn on by a curiosity that was stronger than his own. He swore at her, but fondly. He had been riding since he could walk. There were times when his parents had twenty-five horses and ponies in the yard, buying and selling two or three every week. Out of all the hundreds he rode, he rarely came across one that wasn't noticeably happier when its head was turned towards home. He had never before come across one who point-blank refused to turn back.

He let her go on. They passed a small cottage on the left with a battered van parked outside it. Soon afterwards, the road forked. One branch led into a farmyard, presumably belonging to the cottage. The other, to the right, ended at a little wooden landing stage. Beyond it a dark expanse of water stretched away. There was no bridge. The road went no further.

A boat was pulled up against the jetty; not an elegant pleasure boat but a functional working vessel with greasy water in the bottom. A few yards downriver a concrete slipway led gently down to the water's edge. Beyond that, the bare banks of the river ran into the distance.

The mare stopped dead, her curiosity replaced by a clear anxiety about the dark water ahead. She tried to swing round, but Michael wasn't ready yet. He turned her firmly back. She shook her head hard, wrestled with the bit for a moment, then consented to stand.

There was something about that river. Michael had never seen it before, but he felt that he knew it. Somehow it had always been with him; in him even; a dark thing waiting, like despair, for him to come to it. Stray words passed through his mind.

Wondrous deep . . .
Woe betide you . . .

The mare turned again, but Bandit was pulling in the opposite direction, making for the river; thirsty perhaps. Michael tried to manage the two pairs of reins. It wouldn't be the first time he had been pulled off a horse by the one he was leading. He managed to turn the mare, and was just hauling Bandit back into her side when she stiffened and jumped, and wheeled round to face the way they had come.

Michael dug his heels into her sides, annoyed by her wilfulness. But it hadn't been a ploy. She had been startled by something that he hadn't heard. They weren't alone.

The girl had come up behind him. It was the rustle of her plastic bags that had spooked the mare. And when Michael got a proper look at her, she spooked him as well. She was like someone who had just beamed in from another world. The horses seemed to think so too. All three of them stared.

Michael had never seen anything quite like her. The clothes she was wearing made no sense in the foul weather. They were all black, and tight; everything short and close-fitting. Her hair was an impossible shade of red and her skin, in stark contrast, was waxy and pale. She looked wet and cold.

She walked on past, interested in the horses, not in him. She had rings and studs and bolts all over her face; through her eyebrows, her lips, her ears, her nose.

'Did your mother never teach you not to stare,' she said.

He dropped his gaze.

The mare backed up and began to fidget again. Michael knew he ought to make a start for home, but the girl intrigued him. It was a strange place to encounter someone. There seemed to be nowhere for her to go with all those bags.

He was suddenly aware of how tall he was; how stupid he looked on the little mare. He slipped off.

'Are they your horses?' the girl asked him.

'They are.'

'Why do you have two of them?'

He shrugged. 'I have twenty of them at home.'

'You don't.'

'I do.'

She turned away from him dismissively, as though he wasn't worth talking to. Her arms were stretched by the supermarket bags she was carrying, and where they emerged from her sleeves he could see a number of white scars. He was struck by a vivid image of the girl strengthening herself with steel, then trying to fight her way out of some kind of enclosure. She was battling against razor-wire and carrying the scars.

She walked over to the boat and dropped the bags on to a storage crate.

'Are you going across the river?' he said.

She looked back the way she had come. 'In a wee while. Can I have a ride on your horses?'

'You can't ride in that skirt,' he said. It was so tight

that he couldn't see how she could even walk in it, let alone ride. Beneath it she was wearing black tights and heavy leather boots with big silver buckles.

'I'll take it off then.'

He surprised himself by what he said. 'Go on, then.'

The girl laughed. 'Horses are cool,' she said. 'Will you come another time? I'll wear jeans.'

Michael was enchanted by her laughter. He would probably have agreed to anything she suggested, but at that moment the horses threw up their heads together and looked along the road. Someone else was coming. A woman in a wheelchair, pushed by a man. The woman's lap was laden with more supermarket bags.

'That's my mother,' said the girl.

Michael was trying to think of something to say when the mare, terrified by the sight of the wheelchair, spun round and tried to take off along the river bank. He held on to her, but had to drop the gelding's reins to avoid being torn between the two of them. The mare dragged him along for a few metres before she fetched up against a wooden fence and had to stop. She turned and stared at the wheelchair as if she expected it to pounce on her.

'Fat-head,' he called her. 'Idiot.'

He saw the man begin to step away from the wheel-chair and then hesitate. He was watching the girl, who was quietly approaching Bandit. His reins were trailing on the ground, but the concept of freedom was beyond him. He stood where he was until the girl reached him. She took hold of the reins, and a smile of pride and relief briefly lit her features.

He led the mare back, skittering and jittering across the grass.

'A young man and a grey mare,' said the girl's mother. 'Come to woo our Annie, perhaps?'

The boy blushed, not only because of the woman's suggestion, but because, privately, he had assumed that being in a wheelchair and having a personality were mutually exclusive.

'Look at your Annie,' said the man softly.

The girl was stroking Bandit's nose. The placid cob dropped his head. His eyelids drooped. Annie's confidence was swelling visibly.

'Isn't he gorgeous?' she said.

'He's quiet, anyway,' said her mother. 'I'll say that much for him.'

The boy's dealer instincts surfaced. 'He's for sale,' he said. 'A grand cob. Jump over a Land-Rover, that lad.'

Michael thought it sounded good, but the girl's face clouded over and she glared out at him. The man walked all around Bandit with a very interested sort of look.

'What's your name?'

'Michael Duggan.'

'I don't know any Duggans. From where?'

Michael pointed vaguely in the direction from

which he had come. 'We're new. My mother was born around here. Her name's McLean.'

'Ah.' The man smiled. 'Now I have you. You came down the old road, then.'

'A green track.'

'You must have opened up the gate?'

'We came over it.'

'Hmm.' The man looked more closely at the cob. 'What's he worth?'

'You're not buying him,' said Annie. Her voice was taut and angry. 'You're not buying him for me.'

'No, he isn't,' said her mother.

'I won't be told what I can and can't buy,' said the man. But the mood had changed. A tension had arisen. The woman began to wheel herself towards the boat, and the mare started panicking again. Michael jerked on her bridle, and went to reclaim Bandit and get him out of the way.

Annie released the reins reluctantly, and turned away. But the brief glimpse he had taken into her eyes had been enough to inform him that no matter how hard she had battled with that wire, she had not escaped. She was not free. Unaccountably, Michael felt that he had let her down. All the way home, along the green road, he was troubled by a strong sense of guilt.

He had been out for more than three hours, but no one had even noticed. His mother had gone to get poultices and his father was still where he had been when Michael last saw him: building looseboxes inside the long hay shed.

'Good lad,' he said. 'That pony's looking well. Get Horrocks ready, will you? There's someone coming to see him.'

'I found—' Michael stopped, ambushed by a sudden possessiveness about his track. He didn't want his parents riding along there with him. It was his own.

'What did you find?'

'A river. What river would it be?'

'You'd have to ask your mother. But at a guess I'd say it was the Annan Water. That's the nearest river to here.'

Annan Water. The name sent a cold flush through

Michael's scalp. He had heard it before. Like the river itself, the name seemed always to have been with him, deep in the marrow of his bones.

He didn't hear the car approaching, but his father did.

'Horrocks,' he said. 'Get the mud knocked off him, quick.'

They badly needed money. The move to Scotland had cleaned them out. But Horrocks behaved like a pig and put Frank Duggan in a foul temper for the rest of the day. Michael kept out of his way. He tried to get some information about the Annan Water from his mother, but she was moving too fast. When she got home from Dumfries she was busy boiling kettles and making the poultice for the bay thoroughbred who had got himself tangled up in the remains of an old tractor, and after that she had to ride two young horses before dark. Michael had to ride again as well, and when he was finished he slipped into the cold house before either of his parents could nab him.

He was kneeling in front of the grate, dropping coals onto a pair of firelighters, when he was haunted again by the river.

Annan Water's wondrous deep . . .

It came from nowhere. Words, some vague sense of

a tune or a rhythm.

I loathe that she should wet her feet . . .

He stepped away from the fire and washed his hands in the sink. Then he poured half a stone of potatoes into it and began to scrub them.

I must cross that stream tonight . . .

The image of the tar-black water was so vivid in his mind that he could barely see the potatoes in his hands. It frightened him. He turned on the radio to drown out the invasion. It didn't work.

My love Annie is wondrous bonny . . .

Michael knew about the tricks his mind could play. He had been through all kinds of mental contortions after Joanne died. But it hadn't happened for a long time now. That girl must have got to him somehow.

He dumped the heavy saucepan of spuds on the stove and turned on the heat, then went back into the living room. The firelighters were guttering pathetically. A single coal was smouldering, and the air was full of thin, fumy smoke, as though it had given up the battle against the heavy downslaught of rain in the chimney and retreated into the room.

In the yard, Jean was pouring bags of feed into the steel bins they had brought with them from Yorkshire. Michael ripped into the work beside her.

'I rode down to a river today,' he said. 'Dad thinks it's the Annan Water.'

'Sounds likely,' said Jean. 'How did you get there?'

Michael sidestepped the question. 'Where have I heard of the Annan Water?'

Jean shrugged. 'Geography maybe. In school.'

Michael shook his head. He didn't remember what anyone tried to teach him in school. He had missed too much of it. He wasn't on the right wavelength at all. On the rare occasions that he went, he dreamed the days away. It wasn't hard to stay invisible, when you knew how.

'There's a song or something,' he said.

Jean hefted a bag and nuts rattled into the bin. 'You're right,' she said, remembering. 'There is. My mother used to sing it. She used to sing it all the time.'

Michael opened a sack of oats and poured it into another of the bins. 'How does it go?'

Jean stopped working for a rare moment. She looked at Michael and her lean, weather-tanned face twisted with the effort of dredging her memory. And she was almost there, Michael could tell, when his father's voice reached them from the yard.

'Can somebody give me a hand?'

She was gone from him. Michael carried on with

the work mechanically, but his spirits were dampened. It was always like that. There was never any peace. There were never any quiet, family moments. They were always working. All of them, all the time. For some reason Michael saw an image of the sitting room at the house in Yorkshire. The TV was on, but there was no one watching it. The terrier was polishing off a plate of dinner that had been abandoned on the arm of the couch. That was the way their lives were. They hadn't sat down to a meal together once since they arrived in Scotland. They were a dealer's yard, not a family.

He dreamed about the girl, or about a girl; a face, in a shop like a blacksmith's. A large strong man, whose back was always turned, punched steel rivets and rings into the girl's skin, using a hammer and a massive stapler. The girl's features stretched grotesquely. She didn't seem to feel any pain.

When his mother woke him, he was rigid with fear.

Michael was used to getting up in the dark. He was used to the pre-dawn struggle out into the yard, the hot tea slopping on to the ground, burning his hands on the way. He was used to tacking up sleepy horses in dimly lit boxes. Sometimes he was on automatic pilot, and found himself riding out of the yard with no idea at all of how he had got there.

The three of them were out on the roads at first light, with flashing red bicycle lamps strapped to their arms. Each of his parents rode one horse and led two others. Michael could ride whatever he wanted. He didn't enjoy going out on Bandit, but had chosen him for safety's sake, and he was leading the grey mare. She liked being led. She was quite relaxed when there was no one on top of her.

He had no problems with either of them, but his heart was in his mouth all the same. Both his parents

24

seemed to take a perverse kind of pride in managing the unmanageable. Their horses were all over the road, pulling in different directions, turning the wrong way round, plunging and rearing and dancing, centimetres away from the bumpers of passing lorries. They were like some kind of crazy rodeo act, clattering down the main road, sparks flying from the horses' shoes. Michael swore to himself, over and over and over, as though his anger, his profanities, could protect him from anxiety.

The dream images kept reminding him of the girl, but he had forgotten about the river and the song. His mother hadn't. On the way back, when the horses had finally relaxed and were walking along like a troop of seaside donkeys, she rode up beside him.

'*Woe betide you, Annan Water, By night you are a gloomy river.*'

He remembered the tune as she sang it; remembered his grandmother's voice.

'*And over you I'll build a bridge, That . . . that . . .* Mmm. I can't remember how it goes.'

'It'll come to you,' said Michael. 'It doesn't really matter, anyway. I was just curious.'

'You'd better go to school,' said Jean. 'They'll come looking for you if you don't make an appearance.'

'I don't like that school.'

'You don't have to stay there much longer. Just until the end of the year.'

Michael wished he did like school. His older sister, Fiona, had been an awful lot smarter than he was. She had been an absolutely brilliant rider; better than any of them, his father sometimes said, but she had insisted on going to school; refused to take time off, no matter what was going on in the yard. Michael used to think she was mad, until she got her A levels and left home. Then he realized what it had all been for. Study had been her passport out of the yard. He had left it too late. He didn't have a way out. On the occasions when he allowed himself to think about it, he could see no future for himself beyond home and the horses. He didn't know what he wanted, but he knew he didn't want that.

Woe betide you, Annan Water.

Now that the tune was in his head, other little snatches began to appear.

Annan Water's wondrous deep, And my love Annie is wondrous bonny.

Dum, dum de dum.

Go saddle for me the bonny grey mare . . .

What was it that Annie's mother had said? About a young man on a grey mare?

Frank noticed the time and swore. He put his horses into a steady trot and Michael fell in to the string.

'Come to court our Annie, perhaps.' That was what she had said.

He sat at the back of the class, on his own, near the window. The teacher, a Mr Burns, made several attempts to include him in the discussions, but gave up. They were studying *Macbeth*. It was clear to Mr Burns that the new boy not only had no idea what he was talking about, but had no interest either. It was difficult enough keeping the good pupils involved. There wasn't the time, and there certainly wasn't the energy, to interest the unwilling ones.

'So what's happening here, with the lady, hmm?' he said. 'Has she really fainted, do you think?'

No one answered. After a moment's pause, Mr Burns went on. 'Bit convenient, isn't it?'

Into the silence that followed, the new boy spoke. 'What does "Woe betide" mean?'

'Where's that?' said Mr Burns. 'I can't see where it says that.'

'It doesn't,' said Michael. 'I just wondered what it meant.'

'Well, it means . . . I suppose "woe" is just that. Woe. Sorrow. Misery. Unhappiness. And "betide" – I suppose that means "befall". Or "happen". Woe betide you. Misery attend you. Bad things will happen to you. A kind of warning, I suppose.'

'A warning or a curse?'

'Curse?'

'Is it, like, you know, a hex?'

Several of the other students were snickering quietly.

'Who do you want to hex?' said one of the boys, but Mr Burns silenced him with a glance.

'Well,' he said, 'if I said to you, "Woe betide you if you don't do your homework," it would mean that if you didn't do your homework you could expect trouble to come of it.'

'And if I was a river?'

'You've lost me.'

'He's lost all of us,' said the same boy, and the rest of the class burst out laughing.

'Where did you see it, Michael?' said Mr Burns. 'Why does it interest you?'

But Michael had retreated into his shell again.

'Michael?'

He didn't even look up. Mr Burns sighed and returned to the text.

Michael was riding Horrocks in the jumps paddock. It was almost dark, and he was beginning to fear that the horse couldn't see the jumps properly. But darkness was no deterrent to Frank Duggan. The horse would work until he got it right. Then he would stop, and not before.

'Over the double again, and straight on to the upright.'

The horse was lazy. Michael had to kick like mad to get him going at all, and use his stick hard to keep him moving past the gate. He had to hammer him into the jumps. His father was standing nearby, moving in each time with the long lunging whip at the ready. Horrocks was still reluctant, but he was learning fast.

He took the double well. Loads of scope; it was a shame he was so nappy. Michael was lining him up for the upright when he heard his mother calling him. The horse lifted and sailed out over the jump. Perfect.

'What is it?' he heard his father call back.

'Someone to see Michael!'

Frank sighed and took a long, hard look at the sweating horse. 'He'll do,' he said at last. 'Go on in with him.'

The lights were on in the yard. Someone was leaning against the door of the cow shed, talking to Jean inside. Michael jumped down and led Horrocks past. The person turned to face him. It was the man he had met the previous day, down beside the river.

'Hello, Michael.'

'Hello.' Michael led Horrocks up the ramp of the horsebox. Until his father finished building the new boxes, they were chronically short of space.

Jean appeared at the foot of the ramp. 'You didn't tell me you two had met. I was at school with this gentleman, Michael.'

Michael pulled the saddle and bridle off the horse and closed the slatted gates behind him.

'Jimmy Souter is my name,' said the man.

'Oh.' He dumped the tack in the dingy little dairy, collected a sweat rug and returned up the lorry ramp. Jimmy followed him.

'It was nice to meet you yesterday.'

Michael draped the sweat rug over the horse and threw the heavy jute rug on top of it, upside down.

'Annie liked the horses.'

Jean had already been round and filled the haynets and the water buckets. Michael patted the horse's neck and came out, closing the gates behind him and slipping the steel collar on to secure them. Jimmy followed him down the ramp of the lorry and helped him to close it.

'I was wondering if you'd be interested in giving her lessons.'

'Eh?'

'Annie. Riding lessons.'

'Oh.' Michael glanced towards the lit door of the cowshed, as though expecting his mother to answer the question for him. 'I don't know if I'd be let,' he said.

'You would.'

'When?'

'How about Saturday morning? I'd have Annie ready.'

'Down there by the river?'

'If that's all right.'

It was and it wasn't. The river gave him the creeps, but it enticed him as well. He remembered the dream. He had no idea how to relate to girls.

'I don't really know how to teach.'

'You know how to ride, though.'

'He was riding before he could walk,' said Jean, emerging from the shed and closing the door behind her. 'Will you stay and have a bit of dinner?'

'No,' said Jimmy. 'Some other day I will.' He turned towards his van, which was parked outside the gate. 'Saturday morning, then?'

'I suppose,' said Michael.

'Ten o'clock?'

He started the van before Michael could think of an excuse not to go.

'That's nice,' said Jean.

'Dad'll be livid.'

Beside the hay shed, Frank was fiddling with an electric extension cord. Jean looked across at him. 'I'll fix your dad,' she said.

Michael knew she would, too.

When he got on the bus the next morning he knew he was in trouble. But it wasn't until he walked into the classroom that it hit him. From every corner of the room voices jeered at him. Ghostly voices that whined and wavered. Old people's voices that quivered and creaked. Voices that bleated like sheep.

'Woe betide you. Woe betide you. Woe betide you.'

Michael turned round and went back out of the classroom. He walked down the corridor, ignoring the teacher who tried to stop him, and out of the school. He kept walking until he reached the edge of the town, then he hitched a lift back to the yard.

There was no one around. The lorry was gone. Michael mucked out all the boxes and swept the yard. After lunch he brought a mountain of tack into the cold sitting room and cleaned it all in front of the soaps on TV. After the six o'clock news he filled haynets and carried a bale out to the horses in the field, then came in and made a proper dinner. But his parents didn't turn up to eat it. They didn't get home until eleven o'clock that night. They had been to the sales, sold two horses, and bought three more.

The next day Michael stayed at home. His mother made half-hearted attempts to get him to school, but he ignored her. He was useful to them in the yard. With the best will in the world, it was difficult for them to object too strongly to him being there. Day drifted into day and still Michael didn't return to school. As far as he was concerned, that part of his life was behind him.

He stared into the darkness for hours on Friday night. He couldn't remember the girl's face at all, but he could still see the rings and studs; the criss-crossed scars on her arms. He could see the contempt in her eyes as well; the cynicism. It was something he recognized. It was something they shared.

He tried to bludgeon himself into sleep. He swore at himself; accused himself of cowardice. On difficult horses it always worked; it always made his fear die down, return to wherever it came from. But this time it didn't work. Snatches of the song trespassed on his thoughts throughout the night, and when he did finally sleep they ran through his dreams as well. When he woke at first light there were fragments in his mind and he didn't know whether they were remembered or fabricated by his dream self.

He has ridden o'er field and fen . . .
The sides are steep, the water's deep . . .
The bonny grey mare . . .

The bonny grey mare.

It was a good enough morning. The cloud was low, but not quite low enough to be mist. There was a fine, persistent drizzle, but it wasn't cold. There was no wind at all.

He had planned to take Horrocks and Bandit to the lesson. They were the quietest horses in the yard. He brushed them both till they shone, swearing and shoving at them in their cramped quarters, then tacked them up with the best bridles and the most comfortable saddles. Out in the yard Frank was hosing the leg of a young sport horse with a damaged tendon. He looked up briefly.

'There's a lad coming to look at some ponies,' he said. 'Three o'clock. You'll be back?'

Michael nodded. He mounted Bandit and, leading Horrocks, clattered out of the yard and across the paddocks to the green lane. He tied Horrocks to a fence post and took Bandit over the gate first. The cob pricked his ears and lumbered into it willingly. In the lane Michael slipped off and tied him to a tree. Then he snapped off a stout hazel switch and went back for

Horrocks. His neck was bristling; he was terrified that his father would see what was happening and come storming over to bawl him out of it. He jumped up onto Horrocks and gave him three hard thwacks on the rump. The horse woke up and cantered up to the gate with plenty of attention. But he stopped when he got there, and Michael was on his fourth attempt at it when he was, finally, rumbled.

'What the hell do you think you're doing?' His father had walked out across the fields and was watching him.

Michael said nothing, but began to ride the horse rapidly back towards the yard.

'You've just undone all the flaming work we've put into that flaming horse all week!'

Michael dismounted in the yard and ran up the ramp of the lorry, towing Horrocks behind him.

His father followed. 'And what's the other bugger doing left in the lane?'

Michael dragged the tack off the bay. 'The gate's wired up,' he said.

'Well unwire the flaming gate! Where are your brains, lad?'

Michael walked past him and into the dairy, where he exchanged the tack for a set that fitted the grey mare. Frank followed him to her makeshift box, in one of the narrow cow stalls in the byre.

'And what are you doing taking her out? Didn't I just tell you someone's coming to look at ponies?'

'She'll be better for it,' said Michael.

His father knew he was right. He strode away, still swearing aimlessly, back to his blocks and cement. Michael led the mare out, hosed the worst of the muck off her legs and jumped up. It wasn't until he was well on his way down the green lane, with Bandit happily in tow, that he remembered the main reason he had decided not to take the mare in the first place. His feet reached to her knees. He looked like a fool.

There was nobody waiting for him at the end of the
lane. He rode out past the farmhouse and the fork in
the road, but there was no one waiting at the river
either. For a few awful minutes he thought it was all a
mistake. He had come on the wrong day. The man
Souter had played a trick on him. The worst thought
of all was that the whole thing was a product of his
own mind; a florid fantasy, like the words of the song
which kept creeping up on him, filling themselves in
like a dot-to-dot picture.

Then the girl appeared, behind him.

'You came,' she said.

'Why wouldn't I come?' he said.

She smiled and shrugged.

She was wearing faded black jeans, an anorak and
wellies. She might have looked quite normal if it
hadn't been for all the hardware plumbed into her face.

It hurt him just to look at her.

Jimmy was behind her, pushing her mother in the wheelchair. They were both smiling as if it was Christmas morning.

'I can open the gate into the field there, if you want,' said Jimmy. Michael looked where he pointed, into a flat green pasture. But the mare was already beginning to shift and fuss.

'I think we might be better on the roads the first day,' he said. 'Just till . . .' He felt himself colour. He didn't want to say 'she', and he didn't want to say 'Annie'. Instead he turned to her. 'Until you get used to the feel of the horse.'

The mare shied at the wheelchair again as it approached. Michael slipped off and gave her a talking to, then tightened Bandit's girth.

Annie stepped forward. Michael gave her a leg-up, and while he adjusted the leathers for her, Bandit turned his head and sniffed at her knee. He sighed deeply, as though he had interpreted every atom of her being in that one scenting. He knew her through and through, and Michael was sure he could trust him to take care of her.

'Take the reins like this,' he said. 'Keep your thumb knuckles towards the sky.'

They hacked off up the road, just the hint of the clink of a loose shoe on one of the cob's hind feet. It would last.

'And your heels down. Don't kick him unless you want to go faster.'

'I want to go faster,' said Annie.

Michael smiled. It felt all wrong, as though his face muscles had atrophied. 'Not yet you don't,' he said.

But he had never come across anyone with her kind of courage. By the time they came back from that ride, she was rising to the trot and determined to 'gallop' before she got off. He took her a short way along the green track, letting the cob canter on ahead, even though the mare fizzed like a firework behind him and was in constant danger of striking into his heels. Annie bounced and swayed. Her arms and legs were all over the place, and only a quiet horse like Bandit would have put up with the conflicting messages he was getting. But Annie stayed on, and when they eventually came to a stop, she was red as a beetroot and grinning from ear to ear.

'Again!' She was panting so hard she could hardly speak. Raindrops were falling from her hair into her eyes. He ought to have brought a helmet for her.

'No way,' said Michael. 'You've done enough for one day. I don't think your dad would think much of me if I brought you home in a wheelchair as well.'

Abruptly her face hardened. She gave him a look which he could only try and avoid. He blushed. 'Anyway, you'll be stiff as a post tomorrow.'

'I won't,' said Annie. 'Come on, let's gallop back.'

But Michael was suddenly afraid; not for himself or for the horses, but for her. She reminded him of the grey mare, driven by a recklessness that was barely containable, and could cause terrible damage.

'The horses are tired.' It was a lie.

'Are you tired, Bandit?' she said. The cob cleared his nose in a long, rubbery raspberry. Annie laughed, leaned forward and flung her arms around his neck. Michael flinched, afraid that her studs and spikes would get tangled in the cob's mane. But she straightened up again, safe and glowing.

'Can we do this again?' she said.

'Up to you,' said Michael. 'And your dad, I suppose.'

Annie's face lost its brightness, and he saw again the sullen captive.

'He's not my dad,' she said.

Michael was tightening Bandit's loose shoe when the car drew up. The cob's feet were enormously heavy and, although he was quite mannerly about the process, he didn't offer much help. Michael was groaning and sweating and swearing as he worked.

He heard the car doors slam, and then Frank's voice booming across the yard.

'I'm coming,' he called. He had tightened four of the clenches and there were three to go. He began on another.

'Michael!'

'In a minute!'

He hammered down the next clench, hoping the sound would pass his message to his father. Then he began on the next one.

'Michael?' Frank put his head round the door and groaned. 'I'll do it. Go out with your mother and show them the ponies.'

Jean was in the yard with a woman and a boy. The woman wore similar clothes to Jean: waxed jacket and moleskin jodhs, except that they were much newer and much more expensive. She looked as though there was a smell under her nose that she was determined to ignore. Her son wore the same kind of clothes, and appeared to be on the point of being overwhelmed by the same smell. He hung slightly behind his mother and glared out at Michael with anxious, competitive eyes.

'You'll have to take us as you find us,' Jean was saying. 'We've just made a big move, up from Yorkshire, and as you can see, we haven't really got settled in yet.'

The woman nodded.

'We've a few good ponies in at the moment,' Jean went on. 'Michael's department.'

Michael nodded and swallowed. He hated selling. 'What kind of a pony are you looking for?'

'You said in the ad that you had a Grade A pony. Can we have a look at that one?'

'The grey mare,' he said. 'She's a grand pony; ready to go and make a career for herself. But she's tricky. She's not a novice ride.'

'I'm not a novice rider,' said the boy belligerently. He was probably fourteen; not all that much younger than Michael but a lot smaller and lighter. Michael envied him. He would look just right on a 14.2.

'Let's have a look at her,' said the woman.

Michael tacked up the mare and led her out into the yard. The woman looked her over with an eye that wasn't as practised as she hoped it looked. She felt the mare's legs as though she was a racehorse. The mare kept picking up her feet obligingly.

'She's open to any kind of examination,' said Jean. 'You're welcome to bring a vet to check her over.'

'Let's see what she's like first,' said the woman.

Michael hopped up and walked the mare, on a long rein, towards the jumps paddock. Jean opened the gate and held it while the whole procession went in, then closed it behind them.

As soon as she saw the jumps, the mare began to light up. Michael left the reins loose; let her jog under him, refused to take her bait. The woman asked Jean what her name was. Jean called out to Michael.

'What's her name?'

He had no idea. On paper somewhere she had an official name. Something fancy, made up by her previous owners for the BSJA registration. They always called her the grey mare.

He called out the first thing that came into his head. 'Alice.'

Half the mares in the yard were called Alice. It was one of the names. The fallback name for geldings was Barney.

The long ride that morning had taken nothing out

of the pony. She was as steamy as ever, and as soon as Michael started to warm her up she began to toss her head and plunge around the place. The only way to jump her was to let her bounce along on a very short rein, then line her up at the fence and let her go. Sometimes, riding her, Michael felt like an archer, stretching the bow to a high tension, then releasing it. She never refused, even if she met the fence wrong. She could fiddle her way out of any kind of trouble.

She was jumping high and clean. Michael took her over everything in sight, and Jean put a few of the fences up to really make her stretch. The mare didn't put a foot wrong. When there was no more to show them, Michael took her back to the watchers at the gate. They had to be impressed, but they were doing their best to hide it.

'Do you want to ride her?' the woman was saying to the boy. He looked pale, but he nodded.

'Have you ridden difficult ponies before?' said Jean.

'Loads of them,' the boy said, but he didn't look at her.

Michael could see it would all end in tears. The boy's attitude was too brash. Like a lot of riders, he was substituting aggression for courage. The pony needed lightness and tact. She would make mincemeat of him.

'Try and ride her on a light rein,' he advised. 'Don't hold her in too tight or she'll get fizzy.'

He was wasting his breath. As soon as the mare moved, the boy tightened up the reins and she reacted. She stood on her hind legs and launched herself forward. The boy stayed with her and began to saw at her mouth. She started to froth, and shook her head wildly. He held her in, and she danced on the spot.

Michael was already running to lower the jumps. If the boy tried to take some of the higher ones it could end in worse than tears. Jean saw his intention and, after a brief, cheesy grin to the boy's mother, ran to help. The boy, meanwhile, was trying to get the mare into a steady trot and achieving, instead, a tense kind of sideways canter. The pony's eyes were wide and wild, and her ears were flickering back and forth, searching for the rider's wavelength. He was clearly afraid and she clearly knew it. Michael wished he would admit it and get off. There were other ponies he could try.

They put the jumps down from four foot to two and a half. The boy took three of them successfully. Then he turned towards a double, got a crooked line on it and tried to pull the pony out. She was going too fast, and ended up aiming straight at the wing of the fence. She swerved and jumped at the same time. The boy lost his balance. As he fell he slammed face first into the wing.

Michael closed his eyes, praying that the fall would be clean. He would never forget the sight of his sister being dragged; her head hitting the ground, again and again and again. He would never forget the moment when he realized that she was lifeless; that her pony was dragging a corpse, not a girl.

Jean and the visiting woman were already running forwards. The mare was free, standing with her head over the paddock rail, lifting her knees as though she had half a mind to jump over. The boy was sitting on the ground, his head in his hands. Michael let out his breath and went to catch the mare.

She didn't want to be caught, but he got her in the corner and she submitted. The two women were bending over the boy. With their help he stood up. His face was streaked with blood and tears, but Michael was sure that he wasn't hurt too badly. He had seen plenty of accidents. There was a way people reacted when they were really injured.

The woman must have realized that he was OK as well because, abruptly, she erupted.

'I've a good mind to sue you for this.'

'For what?' said Jean.

'For keeping dangerous animals. Are you insured?'

Michael wished he could evaporate. His mother wouldn't take that kind of stuff lying down.

'How dare you!' she snapped. 'You bring your lad here, give us the impression that he can ride, and end up wasting a lot of our time.'

'He can ride!' the woman shouted.

'Clearly!' Jean shouted back.

'Shut up!' It was the boy, breaking now into hopeless sobs. He was still between the two women, but he burst away from them, wiped his face with his sleeve and ran unsteadily towards his car.

Frank, who had decided to tighten the cob's other shoes while he had the tools out, came to the door of the shed and watched the boy run past, followed by his mother. The car doors slammed. The engine sparked and roared. Michael led the mare back towards her stall.

Jean leaned against Frank, and he put a heavy arm around her. 'We'll never sell that pony,' she said.

'Have we ever failed to shift something?' said Frank. He glanced behind him at Bandit. 'Except for that lad, maybe.'

There were always too many hours in the day and never enough in the night. Other people could lie in bed on Sunday mornings, but for Michael and his family the weekends were usually even more busy than the weekdays. Buyers tended to favour weekends. There was almost always a show. Michael couldn't remember a time in his life when he hadn't been exhausted going to bed; when there hadn't been too few hours left in the night. The only time he hadn't been able to sleep was when Joanne died.

But that night, like the night before, he lay awake for hours. Annie was in his mind. Her pierced and punctured face. Her changing expressions. The dark mood like an undertow to her happiness. What was it he had said that had changed her expression? Something about her father?

More bits of the song came back to him as he lay in bed.

O'er moor and moss and many's the mire . . .

That was why he had liked the song; he remembered now. It was because so much of it was about the horse.

She couldn't have ridden a furlong more . . .

He saw his grandmother's face; heard her voice carrying the words. She had been dead for more than seven years. He had thought her lost for ever from his memory.

. . . Had a thousand whips been laid upon her.
Woe betide you, Annan Water . . .
Woe betide you.

It was a seven o'clock start. Mucking out, grooming, dragging horses into fields and out of them, cleaning tack, loading the lorry. At eight-thirty they snatched a running breakfast, and by nine they were on the road.

It rained all day. The show was indoors, but the practice ring was outside and like a quagmire, full of irritable riders eager to pop their horses over a few fences and get back under cover. It was no place to get a jittery animal settled, and Michael spent a lot of time walking the mare around between the parked lorries and trailers, trying to ease the panic out of her mind. He didn't entirely succeed, but she jumped well enough anyway, and went clear in the first round. She ought to have won outright; there was no pony in the country faster over the ground and tighter on the turns in a jump-off. But Michael spotted the boy who had come to try her in the crowd. He had a black eye and a livid red graze on the same cheek. His mother was beside him, still wearing that expression of distaste.

Michael wanted to win to spite them, and the desire unsettled him and made him lose focus. He let the mare down; pulled her into the double at an impossible angle. She took the first part but there was no chance of straightening out for the second, and they sailed right past it. Three faults, plus all the time it took to come round and face up to the fence again. It put them down into eighth place. Michael kept his eyes turned away from the crowd as he left the ring.

The other pony Michael had brought with him that day might have suited the bruised boy very well. She was a Grade D pony, not as gifted as the grey mare but a great deal steadier. She had come second in her class earlier in the day. Frank, as always, spent most of his show day networking; letting it be known that everything they were jumping that day was for sale. The boy and his mother didn't bite, but someone else did. The pony changed hands on the spot, cash up front. It was a rare enough occurrence, and Frank had to work hard to hide his delight. Two hundred quid went straight off the top of the roll and into Michael's pocket. When there was money he shared it. He was a respected partner in the business.

Bandit jumped a clear round in the horses' D and E, but was outclassed in the jump-off. He always would be. He'd never go on to great things. Jean gave his ear an affectionate tug as Michael slipped off.

'We'll have to get him out hunting again,' she said. 'If he doesn't find an admirer soon he'll end up in a riding school.'

'Or in tin cans with happy dogs on the side,' said Frank.

He wouldn't though. Michael's parents were dealers, and in some way they were hard-nosed. They had to be to survive. But they weren't without scruples. Horses were their livelihood, but they were more than that. Horses were the blood that ran through their veins; the air they breathed; the tireless engines of their dreams. That would never change. Michael knew that beyond the shadow of a doubt, because there had been a moment, just one, when it might have.

It was the day of Joanne's funeral, a year ago, back in Yorkshire. Michael had watched the small coffin descend into the ground and felt nothing. Someone had put a fistful of earth into his hand. It was cold and wet. He couldn't throw it down on to his sister. He let it drop.

He saw everything that happened, but at a distance, removed from himself and his surroundings; but when the family and their closest friends had gathered again at the farmhouse the truth of what had happened began to breach his defences. The house was silent, but there was an awful noise in Michael's head. It was the violent sound of a slamming door, caught at the moment of impact and extended into eternity. It was the crash of a finality which ended nothing but would be with them for ever.

That was the moment. No one had mentioned it,

but the decision was occupying the entire room, exerting an almost intolerable pressure on their over-burdened minds. None of them had slept for days. Michael began to hallucinate. He saw the auction; 450 lots: horses, tack, stable equipment, vehicles. Everything he knew and loved had a paper number glued on to it. He saw himself, beside Frank and Jean, walking away from it all. Into what, his vision did not show him.

Quietly, without a word, Jean broke the tension. She just got up and walked out. A few minutes later, tormented by the continuing silence, Michael went looking for her. He found her in the stable with the pony that had dragged Joanne to her death. Her arms were around his neck and she was crying. She didn't look up, and Michael didn't move or speak, but she heard him anyway; heard the huge booming emptiness that still occupied his mind.

'We'll have to keep him,' she said. 'You can't sell a pony that has killed a child.'

They would have kept him, too; relegated to an ignored retirement, tagging along with the ever-changing stream of horses in and out of the yard and the fields, looking for attention that would never come his way again. But it didn't come to that. The next day an old friend of Frank's, another dealer, arrived in the yard. He bought that pony, and two other 13.2s that Joanne had been bringing on. He paid cash on the nail, top dollar, and took the three away in his lorry.

No one asked what became of them. That man didn't even deal in ponies; only horses. It was the most generous gesture that Michael had ever seen.

By then, of course, the moment had passed. There were horses to be fed and mucked out; exercised and schooled. They had already pulled what remained of the family back into their orbit. The future had returned to its familiar rails and was rattling on into the darkness.

The two horses that Jean had jumped at the show had both been placed. The new rosettes were jumbled up among the string of older ones which stretched across the top of the lorry's windscreen. Beyond them the wipers floated back and forth, leaving drizzling arcs of rain in their wake.

'You should get new blades,' said Michael.

Frank was above their heads, sleeping in the transom that was the bunk for the groom's quarters of the lorry. Wet clothes were heaped up on the middle seat, and the dogs were on top of them, sleeping as well. The heater had begun to make a sinister grinding noise as it battled to keep the big screen demisted. Despite the smell of burning, no heat at all was getting to their feet.

'We should get a new lorry,' said Jean.

'We should get a new life,' said Michael, only half joking.

He turned his attention to the road atlas open on his lap.

'It's the next exit,' he said.

Jean turned off the motorway. There was a series of soft thuds as the horses moved around, adjusting their balance. They were still two hours from home.

Jean waited until they were through the round-abouts and safely on the open road before she spoke again.

'You must go back to school, Michael,' she said.

'I don't see the point.'

'Whether you do or whether you don't, you still have to go. You have to take your GCSEs.'

Michael searched his mind but the same words were still sitting there, jamming up the works.

'I don't see the point.'

He gazed at the road ahead. Raindrops glinted on the top of the glass. His tired eyes blurred them, and he saw the gleam of rings and studs, then the stream of water running down the edges of the windscreen. They drew him in; the dark and the running water.

The sides are steep, the water's deep . . .

He tried to pull the plug on the song, but it wouldn't be silenced. The wiper blades picked up its rhythm, and the white noise of the engine carried the tune.

By night you are a gloomy river.

Mr Burns kept him back after English.

'I've maths next,' said Michael. 'I'll get in trouble.'

'I'll drop you in,' said Mr Burns. 'Don't worry.'

He waited until Michael resigned himself, then sat down on a desk. Michael sat on another near the door, and looked at the littered floor.

'It's a difficult time for you, isn't it?' said Mr Burns.

'No. Why?'

'Moving schools, I mean. In the middle of your GCSEs.'

'Oh,' said Michael. 'I suppose.'

'I haven't seen any of your essays, have I?'

Michael didn't do homework. At his old school they'd given up on him. 'I'll bring them in tomorrow.'

'That would be nice,' said Mr Burns, but Michael could tell he was under no illusions. 'Are you up to date with your reading?'

'I can read fine.'

'I meant your books.'

'Oh. My books.' They were all piled in his locker. He only opened them in class, when the teachers asked him to.

'*Macbeth?*'

'I'll read it tonight.'

Mr Burns laughed. 'You do that. Do you ever read anything else?'

Michael thought about it. At the wall end of the kitchen table there were stacks of show catalogues and magazines, mostly *Horse and Hound*. He glanced through them occasionally. Looking for his name in the show results. Checking out their fortnightly ads.

'A bit,' he said.

'What?' said Mr Burns. 'Papers? Comics? Books?'

There was one book in the house. *Veterinary Notes for Horse Owners*. The cover had fallen off. He'd had an idea of buying a new copy for Jean's birthday. A cold flush went through him. When was her birthday? He couldn't have missed it, could he?

'Michael?'

'Hm?'

Mr Burns sighed. 'There are some books you can buy. They're notes on the set texts.' He wrote the names on a piece of paper as he spoke. 'I don't recommend them normally, but I have a feeling you have a bit of catching up to do.' He handed the page to Michael. 'They practically write the essays for you.'

Michael crammed the paper inside one of his books and made for the door.

It was still there on Friday evening when he came home from school.

'Are you going into town tomorrow?'

Jean was drinking milky coffee in the kitchen, on her feet as always, on her way out.

'I was in today. What did you want?'

'Some books.' He wanted to get the veterinary book as well. Her birthday was a month away, but he was afraid of forgetting again. 'Can we go in again? In the afternoon?'

'There's a show tomorrow. I'll get them for you in the week.'

'You didn't say there was a show.'

'You didn't ask. There's one on Sunday as well. Is something wrong?'

'I was supposed to be giving Annie a lesson.'

'You can put it off, can't you? I don't think there's anything on next Saturday.'

'I'll have to tell her though, won't I? Have you got Jimmy's number?'

'It'll be in the book,' said Jean, and was gone.

They didn't have a phone directory. He tried enquiries, but there were several dozen Souters and he didn't know the address. In the yard the car started up.

He ran out to ask Jean where she was going, how long she would be, whether she could give him a lift to Jimmy's house. The tail-lights of the trailer were already at the gate, and pulled away before he could reach them.

Several of the horses whickered softly as he returned through the yard, but there was still an hour before feeding time. Back in the house, he phoned Jean's mobile. It rang a few feet away, from the pocket of her waterproof, slung over the back of the couch. Michael hung up. The kitchen was warm with bottle-gas fug. He took out a bag of frozen chips and bunged the lot in the oven, then dragged the heater into the sitting room. It was cold and damp. His breath made white clouds around his face. He turned on the TV, then turned it off again and took out his copy of *Macbeth*.

'When shall we three meet again . . .'

He looked at the empty hearth and put down the book. Already the gas fumes were beginning to suffocate him.

The torch batteries were almost spent. The beam was a feeble pale yellow as it roamed across the piles of junk and almost-junk in the loft above the dairy. He could see his bike leaning against the furthest wall. Getting it out was going to be the problem.

There were rustles and rapid patterings underneath the clutter. Michael called the terrier but she couldn't, or wouldn't, come up the steep wooden stairs.

A small tide of irritation quickened his movements. They should have sorted all this stuff out; thrown half of it away instead of carting it wholesale up from Yorkshire. All the broken bits of their lives; the unfixed and the unfixable; the unused and the unusable; the unsold and the unsaleable. There were ripped rugs, snapped head collars, bundles of baler twine. There were job lots of cavessons made from lousy leather, odd riding boots with torn linings, an old ploughing collar with the stuffing bursting out. He began to move things aside. A sackful of drain rods. A felt donkey saddle. The torch beam was fading. Michael called the terrier again, hauled a rotting tarpaulin out of the way. Beneath it was a leaking car battery and a bundle of worn and rusting shoes. Frank always kept them, and never, never reused them.

Michael's temper was rising. He waded further on in, treading heavily, kicking stuff about to scare off the rats. He threw aside a tiny trike with no seat and a burst bin liner, leaking brushing-boots with missing straps. Why had they kept those? He hauled at a bundle of wooden slats and chicken wire that had once been Joanne's rabbit hutch. It collapsed in his hands, but it was the last obstacle; he had cleared the way through. In the last, weak glimmer of light from the torch, he looked at his bike.

Both the tyres were flat.

He grabbed the bike by the crossbar and hurled it across the loft to the trap door. It clattered down the stairs, and there was a yelp as it hit the terrier. Michael followed it, jumped over it, ran into the yard.

'Dad?'

The horses answered hungrily.

'Dad!'

He wasn't there. Michael climbed into the lorry and left the door open to keep the inside light on. He pulled the road atlas out of the side pocket, then rummaged in the tool box under the passenger seat until he found what he was looking for.

The foot pump.

He hadn't ridden his bike for months, and it was suddenly too small for him. The gears kept disengaging when he tried to change them, and after the third time of stopping to put the chain back on, he didn't bother with them any more. The batteries from the radio had powered up the torch again, but once he left the main road he turned it off and only used it when he encountered the occasional car. The night was still with a misty drizzle, which gathered in his hair and ran into his eyes, making them sting.

The map had been clear enough. There was only one road it could be. It was the sound of the river, though, that made him realize that the lights on his right-hand side must belong to Jimmy's house. In the dark, he wouldn't have recognized it.

Jimmy was pleased to see him, but disappointed by the nature of his errand.

'She liked the riding,' he said. 'It meant a lot to her.'

'I can come next week,' said Michael.

'You'd better tell her yourself.'

'I will. Where is she?'

'We'll have to go over.'

'Over?'

'Across the river. They live on the other side.'

Of course they did. The shopping. The boat. How had he ever been stupid enough to think that Jimmy was Annie's father? He must be a friend, helping out, ferrying them across the river and taking them into town. Michael was embarrassed. It should have been obvious from the start. And something else was bothering him as well. Something worse.

'I'll hardly come over,' he said. 'I haven't time. If you give me their number I'll ring her.'

But Jimmy was already getting into his coat. 'It won't take long. I'll give you a lift afterwards. You can throw your bike in the back.'

Oh, boatman, come, put off your boat, Put off your boat for gold and money . . .

'Here, take a turn at the tiller.'

Michael shook his head.

'I'm all right.'

'I know you are,' said Jimmy. 'It sometimes helps. To get a feel for the boat on the water. Calms the nerves.'

Denial surfaced briefly in Michael's mind, as automatic as blinking, then sank again, unspoken. Every inch of him betrayed his terror: his rigid posture on the bench, his white knuckles gripping the side of the boat, his wide gaze locked into the current. It was tugging at something deep inside him, like his half-conscious worries about school, like his grandmother's half-remembered voice.

The sides are steep, the water's deep,
From bank to brae the water's pouring . . .

He couldn't remember the next line, except that it ended with *roaring*.

Roaring. It was all around him like the agitated breath of some water-god bending over the little craft. Closing over his life.

'You might take a wee stroll with the lassie.'

'Hm?'

The roaring was the engine. He could hear no sound from the river above it, except for the slap of the disturbed current against the hull. They were already pulling into the landing stage on the other side.

'I'd like to have a chat with her mother,' Jimmy said.

Annie seemed pleased to see him, and he was pleased to see her as well, although it was some time before his panic finally relinquished its grip on his joints. She didn't question Jimmy's suggestion, but put on a long, black coat with an enormous hood like a monk's cowl. In the outside light on the doorstep the shine of her eyes from its shadows matched the other, metallic glints on her face. Michael couldn't decide how he felt about the piercing. It repelled and fascinated him at the same time.

They walked along the gravelly road, away from the house and the river.

'Why has he packed us off?' said Michael.

'Just to get us out of the house,' said Annie, 'while they get down to a bit of canoodling on the sofa.'

It sounded like a water sport. Canoodling.

'They're both lonely. And they haven't much time left.'

Michael wanted to know more, but so did Annie. 'To what do I owe the pleasure, anyway?'

'Pleasure?'

'What brings you out on a night like this?'

'Oh. I can't make it tomorrow.'

He couldn't see her face, but he could feel her disappointment through all the black layers which lay between them.

'Well, Sunday would be OK.'

'I can't make Sunday, either.'

She turned off the road on to a little footpath, narrower than his own green lane, which ran between hedges of hawthorn and ash. There was no room for two abreast. He walked at her heels.

'Is this the brush-off, then?' she said.

'Brush-off?'

She wheeled on him, pinned him against the wet night which stood behind him. 'Why do you always repeat everything I say? Don't you understand English?'

He fenced at her aggression with his own. 'No. Not a word of it. I'm thick as two short planks, me.'

There was no moon, no stars, but even the darkest

of nights steals light from somewhere. He saw her eyes soften, and a smile touched the corners of her mouth.

'Yeah,' she said. 'And I'm the ghost of Lady Di.'

The hedges ended at a wall with a stile built into it. The track ran along the edge of a bare meadow, and before they were halfway across it, Michael could hear where it was leading them. All his roads that night led to the Annan Water.

They crossed another wall and followed a little bald footpath along the river bank. There were always at least three metres between the path and the river's abrupt edge, but it was never quite enough for Michael. The water's deep song was still summoning him, and the fear was infiltrating his bones again. Annie, walking between him and the bank, vanished abruptly. He thought she had fallen in, but when he looked down he could still see her. She was sitting on something. He felt it in the dark. It was the stump of an old tree; not smooth like a sawn trunk, but uneven, with slimy humps and hollows. There was plenty of room for two to sit there, but Michael didn't fancy it. He stayed on his feet.

'So it's not the brush-off?' said Annie.

'Of course not. I'll definitely be here next Saturday. Definitely.'

'What if I came to you? Would it be easier?'

Michael hated the idea. Annie, his green road, the rare time out: these had already become precious things. But his thought processes were too slow, and hers were too quick.

'Of course it would,' she went on. 'Save you hours. Jimmy could drop me off when he takes her shopping. Pick me up on the way back.'

'I suppose,' said Michael.

'Great! And I can help with the horses. Brush them and stuff!'

Michael wondered what his parents would say. He found it incomprehensible that anyone would subject themselves to that kind of work when they didn't have to, but there were always people, girls especially, who were keen to hang around the yard, for nothing more than the pleasure of being around horses. But Jean and Frank didn't encourage it. They never answered the question that the woman with the smell under her nose had asked. They did not have insurance; never had, never would have. Insurance companies, banks, the Inland Revenue: these were the wolves that stalked their muddy pastures. Michael tried to find a way of explaining it, but it was already too late. Annie's enthusiasm had gathered way too much momentum. There was no turning it back.

'Saturday week, then,' she said. 'I'll be there as early as I can.'

Her bum must have been getting cold and wet from the stump, but she stayed where she was. Michael gnawed at a hangnail on his finger. A rising wind was beginning to blow the soft rain slantways, from one side of the river to the other. The bank was too bare.

'Why are there no trees?' he asked.

'Dunno,' said Annie. 'They say it's that old story. About the young guy who drowned.'

Michael was suddenly sinking with him into the pitch-black tumble of the current; he felt the snag of weeds, the icy touch of a passing fish. He clawed his way back into the night air.

'What story?'

'Just some old story. It's in a song. Ancient. I don't know it.'

There were no brambles, no briars or scrub or weeds. Just the close, rain-battered grass, right up to the lip of the bank.

'I suppose the farmers cut back the bushes,' said Michael.

'I can't wait,' said Annie. 'Can I ride Bandit again?'

As they passed the lighted windows of Annie's house, Michael looked in and saw Annie's mother and Jimmy sitting together on the couch. They weren't engaged in water sports, or anything else energetic. They were just leaning into each other in a still, warm fondness.

'Come and see my room,' said Annie.

Michael left his wellies inside the back door, but Annie pounded up the stairs in her black boots, leaving a trail of mud behind her. The door of her bedroom had 'TREMBLE ALL YE WHO ENTER HERE' written across it in black marker. As she opened it she flicked the switch and a red bulb lit up the room.

Michael had never seen anything like it. Every inch reflected Annie's identity. If he had never met her he would have known her intimately as soon as he crossed that threshold. The floorboards were painted with zebra stripes. The walls, once white, were covered from floor to ceiling with Gothic drawings of dragons and wizards and demon bikers; snatches of poetry, beatitudes and curses, Chinese characters. Everything had been executed by a steady and confident hand, in strong black lines and vivid blocks of colour. A leopard-spotted blanket covered the double bed. Above it, suspended on invisible wires, hung the skull and sweeping horns of a highland cow.

Annie crossed to the black stereo and began to sift through a litter of CDs. 'What do you fancy?'

He was saved from a confession of ignorance by Jimmy's voice, calling up the stairs.

'You ready, Michael?'

Far too soon they were back in the boat again. Every muscle in Michael's body was clenched tight. Pushing their way through the tension, like worms through hard earth, the words of the song wriggled up.

76

Go saddle for me the bonny grey mare,
Go saddle her soon and make her ready,
For I must cross that stream tonight,
Or never more I'll see . . .

He felt a hot flush; a double clench in his tense gut.

. . . my Annie.

As soon as Michael stepped inside the door he remembered the chips he had left in the oven. The black smell in the kitchen told him what had happened to them.

The washing machine was in the middle of the floor, standing in its own guilty puddle. Frank emerged from behind it with a fistful of tools.

'Did you leave the chips on?' he said.

'Sorry,' said Michael.

Frank said nothing. The way they lived, a few burned chips wasn't a bad total for disasters on any given day.

Michael rooted in the fridge but there was nothing remotely edible in there. He pulled a few spuds out of the sack in the porch, but the sink was full of sudsy numnahs and tail bandages. He put the spuds back and went to the breadbin.

Frank stooped down behind the machine again. 'That roan horse is coughing. I put him round the back. Don't let anything near him.'

Michael wrapped a slice of bread around a banana and bit the top off it. 'What's wrong with it?'

'I don't know. Hope it's not a virus, anyway.'

'No. The machine.'

'Oh. Won't empty.'

'Have you checked the filter?'

Frank stood up and assessed the wires and tubes at the back. 'Where is the filter on this?'

Michael opened the little square panel at the front and reached in. A stream of grimy water poured out, along with a 5p piece, a matchstick and half a dozen white plaiting bands.

'Not me,' said Michael. 'I never plait the mare.'

It was after midnight before he saw his bed. He was exhausted, but the sight of his room as he stepped into it brought him up short. If Annie came next week, would he be obliged to bring her up there? He'd seen her room, after all.

The prospect filled him with despair. The windowsill was thick with dead and dying flies. They bred up there, in the roof space, behind the dingy wooden walls. The peeling paint was hospital-coloured. The floorboards were rough and bare. Apart from his bed and the clothes piled on two wooden chairs, the room was empty. No stereo, no posters, no comfort. The place was a proclamation, not of his personality, but of his lack of it. He had made no imprint upon it at all.

He tried to think about it as he lay in bed, waiting for the rucked sheets and blankets to trap his heat for him. But he had no idea where to start, and before he had come up with anything the song began to invade him again.

For I must cross that stream tonight, Or never more I'll see my . . .

He slammed his head into the pillow to shut it out. And suddenly, it was morning.

The Saturday show was a local one – only half an hour away in the lorry. They had the whole morning at home, and Michael was gutted by the knowledge that Annie could have come and ridden after all, if he'd known. But, as always, there was no time to dwell on things. His mother's trip of the previous evening had resulted in a trailer piled high with golden barley straw, which had to be unloaded and stacked in the one bay of the hay shed that wasn't full of breeze blocks and half-built walls.

Jean had kinks to iron out of one of the horses she was taking to the show, so Michael took over her veterinary duties for the morning. He changed the poultice on the thoroughbred's hock, then investigated the lameness that had developed in one of the new horses Frank had bought at the sales. He found heat in the foot, took the shoe off, excavated with a hoof knife until a pus-filled pocket discharged most of its contents in a powerful jet across the loosebox.

'Found it,' he called to Frank, who was passing with a laden wheelbarrow.

'Found what?'

'Puncture wound, I'd say.'

Frank came in and examined Michael's work. 'Good man. Could have been a vet, you.'

'Could have,' Michael thought, as he dug out the grungy old poultice boot from the bottom of the trunk in the tack room. 'Could have' still needled him as he scalded another poultice and carried it steaming across the yard to the box. The horse tried to snatch its foot away from the sudden heat, but Michael hung on. He wrapped a plastic bag around it, secured it with two elastic bandages and strapped the rubber boot on over it all.

Why not 'could'?

The answer was clear enough. Because he didn't understand the questions in his maths class, let alone the answers. He hadn't opened a biology book that term, and he didn't even seem to have chemistry on his timetable. Being a vet meant top marks, A levels, years in college.

Frank was right. He could have been a vet. If.

The boy's eye was still slightly black, but the graze had healed over completely. He was in the collecting ring when Michael spotted him, riding the bay mare they had sold the previous week, to someone else.

The pony, just as the grey mare had been under that boy, was full of uncertainty. Her ears twitched back and forth, waiting for the clear signals that Michael had taught her, failing to receive them. But her heart was good; she jumped everything she was faced at, putting herself right when the boy got things wrong, doing her level best.

They might have gone well enough in their class, if the rider hadn't forgotten the course, jumped two fences in the wrong order and got himself disqualified. He came out of the arena red-faced with embarrassment, rode the bewildered pony back into the practice ring and drove her viciously over the jumps again. It was only the pony's good sense that kept him out of the trouble he was asking for.

Michael's young chestnut took the back bar off a parallel, but it was only his second time out and he was pleased with him. Later in the day, the grey mare won her class, and a man with a fifteen-year-old daughter showed some interest in her. Frank took over the haggling, but the deal fell apart when he refused to let them take the mare on a fortnight's trial.

'I've had horses handed back to me on their knees,' he told the man. 'You could take that chestnut pony for as long as you like, and he'll be half the price. But not this one.'

Michael had heard it all before. He knew what Frank's mood was like when he lost a sale like that, and he took the mare, still wearing her red rosette, back to the lorry.

The Sunday show was a disaster. There were no pony classes, so Michael had brought Bandit and a lanky little black horse called Oliver to go in the D and E. Neither of them jumped well. Jean's best horse, The Menace, overreached and injured himself in the practice ring and she had to withdraw him from the Open. Her other Open horse spooked at a child with a balloon on a critical turn and ploughed through the next pair of fences. They came home, for once, ribbonless.

It was late when they got back, but Jean put on a proper dinner while the others unloaded the horses and tack, and settled the yard for the night. If she hadn't tried to light the fire, the meal would have been perfect. As it was, the whole house was full of smoke, and they had to eat in the freezing draughts from the open door and windows.

After dinner Michael took his school bag to his room. He had piles of homework and had meant to do it all. But the words stayed stuck on the pages of his text books. No matter how hard he tried to concentrate, they wouldn't make the transition into his head. He could read them, even speak them, but he couldn't make them work for him.

Later, in the windswept night, the books woke him as they fell from his bed on to the floor.

Between a flat car battery and a broken fence which let seven horses out on to the main road, Monday got lost.

On Tuesday Jean and Michael went drag hunting on Bandit and Horrocks. Michael hated the high boots, the fussy stock and the new hacking jacket. They made him feel like a fool. But he loved the mad, muddy charge across the landscape, the neglect of sinew and bone in the rush of recklessness as they leaped and plunged and scrambled over every obstacle they encountered.

After that, on Wednesday, school was an ignominy. The other lads had tired of the 'woe betide you' taunt. It hadn't produced the desired result. Instead they relegated Michael to the edges of everything: their groups, their fields of vision, their boisterous lives. There were other boys out there with him in that no-man's-land of otherness. Like him, they endured.

* * *

'No essay for me?' said Mr Burns, walking backwards up the classroom, gathering the homework.

'I left it at home,' said Michael.

'Bring it in tomorrow.' Mr Burns passed on.

The bell rang. The class broke up and bolted for the door. Michael drifted after them. The bustling corridors were lined with paintings, team photographs, club notice boards.

But, like his bedroom, the school bore no record of Michael's existence.

On Saturday morning, when they clattered into the yard from their roadwork, Annie was waiting. She was wearing her black jeans and a neat, black bomber jacket with a huge red butterfly painted on the back. She waved up at Michael, but his hands were too full of reins to wave back.

She helped him. She came and held Oliver while he put away the grey mare, then insisted on leading him across the yard to the narrow shed where he was billeted. Michael showed her how to do it properly; to walk at the horse's left shoulder instead of in front of him.

'Save your good boots,' he said. 'And the good feet inside them.'

She took the tack off as well, following Michael's instructions deftly; learning quickly. There was an eagerness about her; a delight in the simplest and most mundane of equine things. It surprised him. Perhaps she needed the funereal clothes and all that iron-mongery to hold her down. As though, beneath it, she was as light and as translucent as a spirit.

She followed him to the dairy and pounced on the grooming box. 'Can I brush him?' she said. 'Or Bandit? Can I brush Bandit?'

There were muscles in Michael's face that he had forgotten about.

'He smiles!' said Annie. 'Lo and behold!'

'You can brush anyone you like,' he said.

'You'll wish you hadn't said that.' She pursued him across the yard with the body brush until he collided with Jean and the two of them went down beneath her armload of tack.

'Sorry,' said Annie, pulling the three bridles into a hopeless tangle. 'Sorry.'

But Jean was laughing. She twisted Michael's arm behind his back and wouldn't let him up until Annie got her way with the brush.

They rode in the field, Annie on Bandit and Michael on a young Irish sport horse that Jean had just finished breaking. He had a brilliant pedigree but an accident in the lorry coming over had left him with a pair of capped hocks and brought him within their budget. They had high hopes for him.

Michael had dug out one of his outgrown skull caps for Annie. She looked good in it, with her scarlet hair curling out around its frame. She wanted to gallop and jump, but he made her stick to the basics: stopping and starting, circling at a walk and a trot. He did the same things himself, and by the end of the hour he was well satisfied with his teaching. Annie was dropping her hands. The sport horse was dropping his head. Everyone was making contact. He called a halt while the good notes held.

It was colder inside the house than outside it. Michael put the kettle on and lit the gas heater.

Annie hugged herself and wandered into the sitting room. 'Shall I light the fire?' she said.

'It won't light,' said Michael. 'The smoke comes back.'

He rummaged for biscuits. Annie was on her knees in front of the fireplace, peering up the chimney.

'It's blocked, that's all,' she said.

'I suppose we'll call in a sweep some time.'

'Have you no chimney rods?'

Chimney rods.

'Aren't they the same as drain rods?' said Michael.

There was no brush with the rods but they improvised with two dandy brushes wired on back to back. Annie showed how it was done, feeding the first two rods up the chimney then screwing on the third one and pushing it on up. After five, maybe six lengths, the progress of the brushes was halted.

Annie pulled back an arm's length of the rods and gave a shove. A blackened twig dropped into the grate.

'There's your problem,' she said.

'That was hardly blocking it,' said Michael.

'Jackdaws,' said Annie. 'They build dirty great beaver dams for nests. Wait till you see.'

She rolled up her sleeves, and Michael saw the ranked scars. Some of them were still pink, still healing. Annie saw him looking.

'I cut myself,' she said.

'Why?'

She shrugged and, with ferocious energy, began to ram away at the blockage in the chimney. Her strength surprised him, but apart from another small trickle of broken twigs, she wasn't getting anywhere.

When she stopped for a breather he took over. It felt to him as though he was thumping away at something much more substantial than twigs.

'Can't be just a nest,' he said.

'Bet you it is.' Annie took the rods back, and for the next few minutes they took it in turns to assault the obstruction. More twigs fell. A small, downy feather. A few wisps of dried grass. Then, without warning, the whole lot came down. The grate was buried in sooty sticks and dust. They both stepped back, waiting for the avalanche to subside and for the soot to settle.

'You'll have kindling there for a month,' said Annie.

Michael was busy with the hearth brush and Annie was tying up the rods again when Frank came in, dripping blood and looking for plasters.

'Kettle's boiling,' he said. 'My God. A fire. How did you do that?'

Annie helped Frank bind up his bleeding thumb, and Michael went to call Jean in from the yard. When she came in she found the sofa and armchairs pulled up to a roaring fire, and a pot of tea brewing on the hearth.

She shoved a dog aside and sat down. 'You should come here more often,' she said to Annie.

After lunch, Michael and Jean rode Horrocks and Oliver in the paddock. Annie helped Frank with the jumps. They were just returning to the yard when Jimmy and Ruth arrived in the van.

Annie was reluctant to leave. 'Can I come again tomorrow?' she said.

'We have to go to a show,' said Michael.

'Can I come? Pleasepleaseplease?'

'Of course you can,' said Jean. 'If you don't mind squashing up in the lorry.'

Annie squealed, danced over to the van and dived in. 'What time?' she called through the window.

'Eight o'clock,' said Frank.

Annie waved at them until she was out of sight.

'Wow,' said Jean.

'Wow,' said Frank.

A hot surge of joy raced through Michael's blood. He wanted to climb the house, stand on the liberated chimney stack, broadcast Annie's name to the four corners of the world.

Those forgotten muscles had locked themselves into a foolish grin. To conceal it from his parents, Michael turned and sprinted back to the house.

Annie bent over backwards to make herself useful at the show, but most of the time she got in everybody's way. She didn't understand the routines, the urgencies and overlaps, the acute concentration required by everyone to make sure that the right horse was ready at exactly the right time. She pestered Michael with questions, dividing his attention, taking his eye off the ball. She fetched things that hadn't been asked for, got on the wrong sides of horses, ropes, partitions; brought cups of tea when no one had time to drink them.

It wouldn't have been so bad if Michael had been able to ignore her. But he feasted on her bright presence; he couldn't take his eyes off her. His face was permanently set in that goony grin.

His parents' tolerance lasted until he almost missed his turn in the first class. They found him sitting on the chestnut pony outside the arena, chatting dreamily to Annie, while his name was being called inside.

It knocked the smile off his face. He tore through the waiting riders into the ring and made it just in time. But the panic had unsettled the pony. They had two fences down.

'Sorry,' said Annie, as he came out. 'Sorrysorry-sorry.'

The smile stole up on him again.

The black eye was gone, but the black attitude wasn't. As soon as the boy came into the arena, Michael could see what was about to happen. The bay pony was stiff with apprehension. Her mind was anywhere and everywhere, except on the job. After the first refusal the boy belted her three times with the stick. After the second, the pony bolted across the ring before she could be hit again. They narrowly avoided elimination.

Even Annie noticed.

'The little bollocks.'

'That was one of ours,' said Michael. 'We sold her a while back.'

He wasn't the only one to have remembered that. A few minutes after the boy's undignified exit, his mother appeared on the scene.

'You must be delighted with yourselves,' she said.

'I beg your pardon?' said Jean.

'You managed to palm that one off on us.'

Frank was watching the pony in the ring, but he

had heard. He swung round. The colour was rising to his cheeks. 'Excuse me,' he said. 'I don't remember selling you anything.'

Her husband emerged from the crowd at the appropriate moment. 'You sold it to me,' he said.

'I did,' said Frank. 'But I wouldn't have if I'd known who she was going to.'

'What exactly are you saying?'

The atmosphere was becoming brittle. Michael noticed that Annie was reversing quietly in behind him. Frank squared up to the man. 'I'm saying your boy wants a few lessons. There's nothing wrong with that pony.'

'You've always got an answer, haven't you? Someone else's fault. Bloody dealers!'

He took his wife's arm and made to move away, but Frank wasn't finished.

'No, no,' he said. 'I'm not having that.' He jerked his thumb towards the exit. An elastoplast was hanging off it. 'Come here with me.'

Annie was at Michael's shoulder. He could feel her tension through the light contact where her clothes touched his.

'Oh, no,' she whispered.

But Michael knew that Frank wasn't proposing a fight. He had something else up his sleeve.

Michael, shadowed by Annie, went back to the lorry,

put away the chestnut and tacked up the grey mare, ready for the Open. He was just starting to warm her up in the practice ring when Frank called him over to the fence. He was leading the bay pony.

'Hop up on this lady,' he said. 'I got them to enter her in the Open for you.'

'In the Open! She's only got half a dozen points!'

'Come on, Michael.' Frank was serious. 'We can't take that kind of crap from the likes of them.'

Michael sighed, slid down from the mare and swapped his saddle over. From her perch on the wooden rails, Annie was watching. Michael's stomach turned. It was do or die. Get the pony back on the rails or make almighty fools of them all. It would have been bad enough without Annie's admiring gaze. Her presence put an extra, almost unbearable pressure on him.

He vaulted up and rode into the practice ring. He could hardly believe it was the same pony. She was edgy and hesitant, no longer sure what any of his instructions meant. She was carrying her head way too high, and her ears were directed towards him, instead of the rest of the world. She showed all the signs of a very frightened pony.

He walked, trotted, turned, bent the pony this way and that. He made her think; made her concentrate. Inside ten minutes she was beginning to remember him; relaxing between his light hands and firm, reassuring heels. She lowered her head and began to move more freely. Her ears faced forwards for longer and longer spells.

Michael was pleased with her progress. He glanced up, hoping that Frank was watching. He wasn't, but the boy's parents were. And Annie. Where was Annie?

When he saw her, the shock he got made him pull the pony to a stop. Sometimes he thought that Frank was mentally damaged. He had put Annie, bareback, up on the grey mare. She was walking her around among the mêlée of riders charging backwards and forwards between the practice area and the collecting ring. He started for the exit, then stopped again.

Annie wasn't the only one who was happy. The mare was mooching around, plucking the odd blade of grass out of the mud, as relaxed as if she was in a summer meadow. Absurdly, it was Annie's ignorance that was keeping her safe. She was as happy and calm as could be, twiddling the mare's short mane; talking, maybe even singing, to her.

Michael turned back to the job in hand. He had a lot to do in the next twenty minutes.

By the time his turn came to jump, he had ironed all the hesitancy out of the pony and got her back on an even keel. But he was under no illusions. It was asking a lot of a novice pony to jump an Open course.

Jean had put her own saddle on the grey mare and was warming her up again. Annie was waiting with

Frank in the passage. She stepped forward and patted the bay pony as Michael went past.

'Show 'em how it's done,' she said.

His heart sank. She had no idea.

But the pony amazed them all. Her confidence was restored. Her concentration was perfect. She listened attentively to Michael and responded instantly to his every signal. When they cleared the last of the eleven fences, a single high-pitched cheer rose above the scattered clapping.

Michael blushed. He had a fan.

'I'll buy her back off you,' Frank was saying to the boy's parents as Michael jumped down. 'I'll give you a hundred pounds profit.'

They glanced at each other. The man shook his head. They were already leading the pony away as Michael retrieved his saddle.

'Two hundred pounds!' Frank called after them. 'Two hundred and fifty!'

But they were gone, and he was laughing. He cuffed Michael affectionately. 'Good lad,' he said.

Michael's spirit swelled, but it was nothing compared to how he felt a few minutes later. Annie walked with him towards the practice area, to take the grey mare from Jean. The rain had started again. Neither of them noticed.

'You know what you are?' said Annie.

'No?'

'A bloody genius, that's all.'

He couldn't remember a time when he hadn't been jumping in shows. Winning still gave him a buzz; it was what it was all about. But nothing in his life before had ever made him feel as good as Annie's praise.

And that was only the beginning. The grey mare bounced and battled her way into first place, and brought the girl and her father back to have another look at her afterwards.

'The price has gone up,' said Frank. He was in high spirits. 'It'll go up again next week.'

The girl looked crestfallen and her father groaned.

'It's just that we've been warned,' he said. 'Not to buy anything without taking it on trial first.'

'It's good advice,' said Frank. 'I can't help you, though. You can take a spin on her now, if you like. Or come and ride her at our place. Every day for a fortnight, if it suits you.'

The man shook his head and walked away. Michael watched as, out of earshot, he entered into a long argument with his daughter. Eventually they came back and took Frank's name and address. Frank winked slyly at Annie.

Bandit, cheered on frantically by Annie, went clear in the first round. He went clear again in the jump-off, but hopelessly slowly. It wasn't enough to get him in the money, but he collected a pink ribbon, which Michael gave to Annie.

She couldn't have been more thrilled if she had won it herself. 'I'll hang it on the cow's horn,' she said. 'My first departure into pink.'

'Do you want a red one instead?' Michael asked her.

'Not unless Bandit won it,' she said.

'That'll be the day,' said Michael.

He let her ride Bandit back to the lorry.

'Look at me,' she said. 'I mean, just look at me! I'm at a horse show, riding a horse. I just can't believe it!'

Michael was besieged by a series of vivid images. Annie jumping Bandit over cross-poles. Annie jumping in shows. Annie beside him in the yard, in the house, around the fire . . .

His thought process stalled. He had been glacial for far too long. The sudden meltwaters threatened to carry his mind away on their tide.

'You look great up there,' was all he said. 'You look the part.'

The Menace was still lame. Jean had only one to go in the Open, and he was already off the lorry, getting warmed up. Michael and Annie got the others settled with their haynets and went into the little groom's compartment. There were sandwiches and chocolate bars and flasks of sweet, milky coffee in there.

'This is brilliant,' said Annie. 'You could live in here.'

'You could, I suppose,' said Michael, glancing at the bunk above the transom.

'I could,' said Annie. 'Maybe I'll rent it off you. How much?'

Michael laughed, but something had happened. A shutter had fallen behind Annie's eyes. She was miles away from him, as dark and distant as the first time he had seen her.

'I'm not staying at home, anyway,' she said. 'Not once my dad comes home.'

'Your dad?' said Michael. 'Why? Where is he?'

Her right knee was suddenly in frantic motion. The heel of her black boot hammered on the frayed matting. She looked up at him. Ravens lurked in her dark eyes.

'He's in prison,' she said. 'I put him there.'

Michael couldn't believe he could come down so quickly. Even the sky seemed to be collapsing outside the open door, as the mist and the night fell together.

'Why?' he said. 'What did he do?'

Annie didn't answer. She was so far gone from him that he needed her name to call her back.

'Annie?'

She looked up, hard still.

'Are you OK?' he said.

She shrugged. Her knee had stopped jerking. She sighed, softened a bit. 'I'm supposed to go down there for a couple of days next week with my mum.

Counsellors and all that crap. I've been there. Done that. No way am I going again.'

'Maybe you should go?' said Michael. 'Tell them how you feel.'

She shook her head. 'I want him to come back. He's promised to look after Mum. She wants him back so I don't have to be tied down because of her MS. She thinks if he comes back I'll forgive him and we'll all be a happy family again. I won't, though. I'll never forgive him.'

Michael's head was full of questions that he didn't feel he could ask. How long had he been in prison? What had he done to her?

'Will you really leave?' is what he said.

Annie nodded. 'I won't set foot in the house once he comes back. Never.'

'Where will you go?'

'I dunno. Out of Scotland, anyway.'

The mist seemed to be pushing in through the door, but Michael couldn't seem to find the will to close it. Instead, they both sat in silence, immune to the surrounding contentment of the munching horses.

They had to crawl home through the dense mist. Jean and Frank took turns to sleep in the transom. Michael and Annie sat side by side in the double passenger seat. He ached to put his arm around her, take her head and all its sorrows on to his shoulder. In the end it was he who nodded off and slumped towards her, and woke when the lorry bumped over a railway crossing and knocked their skulls together.

It broke them out of their gloom. Frank started singing the only song he knew. '*One man went to mow . . .*'

Annie joined in. They giggled and sang the rest of the way home.

When they got back, Annie helped Michael to carry haynets and water buckets around the yard. While she was kissing Bandit good night, an idea occurred to him.

'Why don't you stay here?'

'Your mum said she'd drop me home.'

'No, I don't mean tonight. I mean next week. When your mum's away.'

She looked up at him. He could tell she wanted to. 'What about your folks?'

'Oh, they're cool. They like you. It won't be a problem.'

'I might,' she said. 'I'll ring you.'

He squatted on the damp cobbles and carved his phone number with a hoof pick on a broken piece of slate. Frank passed by, a bale of straw on his back.

'Be sure and come back now, you hear?' he said to Annie. 'As soon as you like.'

'See?' said Michael. 'I told you.'

He dreamed that the jackdaws were back, pouring concrete down the chimney. He was trying to swim through it before it set when he woke. The song, and that old, dead stump, were lurking in his mind.

Woe betide the willow wan,
And woe betide the bush and briar,
For they broke beneath her true love's hand,
When strength did fail and limb did tire.

He was amazed that those lines had taken so long to return to him. They were the ones that he had waited for every time his grandmother sang it; that had made the blood rush up his spine, even as a small child. They were doing it again now. There was another one as well. What was it?

It wasn't just the river that was condemned, then. That was why the banks were bare. It must have been that stretch of water the young man tried to cross. He nearly made it, but the growing things failed him. They broke away as he tried to struggle out, and they had been cursed for it. Every one of them had died, and never grown again.

He tried to find his reason. It couldn't possibly be true. It was just a song, just a coincidence. But the hour was against him. He was still half in the dreamtime, and the song ran on through him. It was no longer his grandmother's voice that carried it. Somehow, he didn't know how, it was the river's.

As soon as he got up, it was in his mind that Annie might ring. It was in his mind even at school. He was lifting the phone, trying cool, then surprised, then delighted, when he was ambushed by the maths teacher.

'You're looking very cheerful there, Michael,' she said. 'Finished those problems?'

He put his face back into neutral. 'No, miss.'

She began to walk towards his desk. He checked his neighbour's book for the page number and opened his copy.

'A pen might help,' said the teacher.

Michael felt the colour in his cheeks. He poked around in his bag.

The teacher sighed. 'It's up to you,' she said. 'All of you. I can't programme you. If you don't do the work you won't pass the exam. It's as simple as that.'

Michael leaned on his elbows and scratched his head. Something grey and scrofulous dropped onto the white page. He picked it up on the tip of his pen and scribbled it into a clean corner. It must have come out of the body brush when Annie caught up with him on Saturday.

He locked his jaw so that his face couldn't betray him again, and surrendered to the memory.

She phoned on Wednesday evening.

'Is it still all right to stay with you?'

'Yeah,' he spluttered. 'Definitely.'

'Tonight? Until Saturday?'

'Brilliant!'

'Jimmy says he can drop me over in a while. He'll mind my mum and drive her down tomorrow.'

'Brilliant,' he said again. 'Come whenever you like.'

He wandered out into the yard. Frank was in the hay shed, making doors for the new boxes.

'Annie's coming over,' said Michael.

'Now?' said Frank.

'For a couple of days.'

'A couple of days?'

'Her mum's going away.'

Frank examined a nail underneath the dangling bulb, then hammered it into the door. 'How'll you manage with school and all that?'

Michael shrugged. 'It's only a couple of days.'

Frank dug into the nail bucket again. 'How are you doing, anyway?'

'Oh, grand.'

'Keeping up all right?'

'Yeah. Fine.'

Frank hammered again. 'No, it's just . . . I got a phone call the other day. We seem to have missed some meeting or other. Parent-teacher.'

Michael nodded. 'I gave you the letter.'

'Did you?'

'It doesn't matter, anyway. Most of the parents didn't bother.'

'As long as you're doing all right.'

'I'm doing all right.'

Michael went back to the house and retrieved the crumpled letter from the bottom of his bag. He smoothed it out as well as he could and pushed it into the middle of the paper stack at the end of the table. He sifted through it. There were bills with FINAL NOTICE plastered across them. A car tax renewal form. Catalogues for shows and sales. Entry forms, some half filled in. Registration documents from the BSJA. They had no filing system. This was it.

He fingered the notes in his pocket uneasily. He took a share of the profits, but he also shared the liability. The unpaid bills made him anxious. It wouldn't be the first time that he would see his money swallowed up by the running of the house and yard.

There was a bag of baking potatoes on the counter. He turned on the oven and threw six of them in. Then, as a joyful afterthought, he threw in two more. He changed into his mucky jeans and went out to start on the yard, but the van was already there. Frank was leaning into the cab, talking to Jimmy and Ruth. Annie was walking towards him, carrying two bulging carrier bags.

'Gross,' said Annie, when she saw his room. 'We'll have to do something about this.'

'Fine by me,' said Michael. 'When do we start?'

'Got any paint?'

'I can get some tomorrow.'

'Tomorrow, then,' said Annie. 'We start tomorrow.'

He showed her to the spare bedroom next door and dredged though the unsorted chaos of clothes in the airing cupboard in search of clean sheets and blankets. When they'd made up the bed they clattered back down to the kitchen.

Frank was sitting at the table. He looked up as they came in. 'Everything all right?'

'Brilliant,' said Annie.

Frank galloped his fingers on the table for a moment. 'I'm sorry about your mother,' he said. 'I didn't realize.'

'She could be worse,' said Annie. 'She's in remission.'

Frank nodded, but Michael could see the recent shock still present in his eyes. It was more than Ruth's condition, he was sure of that. They had told him something else as well.

'I didn't realize,' he said again. 'Be sure and make yourself at home.'

They were all downstairs before dawn; Annie pale and bewildered by the early start. But the prospect of a ride drove all else from her thoughts, and she was soon firing on all cylinders and eager to be off.

'Do you sleep in all that chandlery?' said Frank. 'Doesn't it get tangled up in the bedclothes?'

Michael signed the hand-me-down skull cap over to her. 'It's yours,' he said.

'Class!'

She turned it between her hands and Michael could see her mind working. It wouldn't be long before that helmet bore Annie's mark. A death's head. A line of Japanese characters. A fresh coat of black paint with red pinstripes. It would be indisputably hers, then. In all the years Michael had owned it, it had acquired none of his personality at all, apart from a few scrapes and chips.

'You'd be as well to get a new one,' said Jean. 'If you're going to take riding seriously, that is. They say you should replace them if you drop them.'

'That one's been dropped a hundred times,' said Frank.

'Yes,' said Jean. 'And usually with Michael's head inside it.'

'You serious?' said Annie. 'Have you fallen off?'

'You've got to be joking!' said Michael. 'I come off at least once a week. We all do.'

'Speak for yourself,' said Frank.

'You would too, if you ever did more than road-work.' He turned back to Annie. 'It's part of the job.'

Annie looked disappointed.

'Never mind,' said Frank. 'Come out and see if you can do it too.'

She didn't, though. Bandit took good care of her, bringing up the rear of the rambunctious ride, keeping well clear of the fireworks. Michael glanced back from time to time, but Annie seemed to be in no need of reassurance. On the contrary, she was having a ball, and fast becoming a rider.

After breakfast they loaded the roan horse and a leggy two-year-old that none of them liked on to the lorry. Frank was off to the sales with them, and he dropped Michael and Annie off in town on his way through.

'Don't be bringing them home again, you hear me?'

said Michael, as he jumped out over the wheel arch. 'Nor any new ones, either!'

'Why not?' said Annie, as they ducked into a shop doorway to shelter from the rain.

'Too many horses,' said Michael.

'Naa,' said Annie. 'No one could have too many horses.'

They bought brushes and scrapers and turps and sandpaper; a gallon of white gloss and a half gallon of black. Annie chose it all, and Michael paid. His roll of notes impressed her.

'Where did you pilfer that?'

'I earned it,' he said. 'My share of the sales.'

'Wow,' said Annie. 'Wow!'

They left the paint to collect later, and went on to a bookshop. Michael found the study notes easily enough, but there wasn't a copy of *Veterinary Notes for Horse Owners*. He was disappointed.

'When's her birthday?' asked Annie.

'Not until the twenty-eighth.'

'Order it, then. There's plenty of time.'

She marched up to the counter. The assistant looked up the book on the computer.

'It's in print,' she said. 'We should have it inside a week.'

'Can you post it to me?' said Michael.

'We can. You'll have to pay the postage.'

'Can you gift wrap it?' said Annie.

The assistant smiled. 'Whatever you like.'

'We'll get a card,' said Annie. 'Get the whole thing sorted. They can post it straight out to Jean if you tell them the right date.'

They chose a Gary Larson cartoon and Michael borrowed a pen to write in it, then handed it on to Annie. 'You sign it too.'

'No. It's from you.'

'From you too. Go on.'

Annie took the pen and signed the card in her stylish calligraphy. Michael sealed it and handed it over to the assistant, who took all the details and rang up the total on the till. Michael was walking on air as they left the shop. Jean's birthday was taken care of. It was a weight off his mind.

'How did I ever survive without you?' he said.

Annie linked her arm through his and squeezed it. They broke into a spontaneous soft-shoe shuffle along the pavement, and the Dumfries shoppers parted before them.

They sat in a café over tea and buns, and afterwards Annie dragged Michael in to get an ear pierced. As soon as he'd got it done she said, 'Shall we go the whole hog? Shall we get a tattoo?'

He shrugged. He would have followed her through a butcher's mincer if she had asked him to.

She got a Celtic cross in black and red, and picked out a caduceus for him: two snakes entwined around an ivy-clad stick.

'It's something alchemical,' she said. 'Only for geniuses.'

'Where's yours, then?'

'That's what you'd like to know, isn't it?' she said, and the look she gave him hit him somewhere in the solar plexus.

The needles hurt more than he expected them to, and Michael had to keep reminding himself to stop looking. Instead he watched the other tattooist working on Annie. He noticed that the pink scars were fading; blending into the white web, and that there was no sign of any new ones. He hoped it meant she had given up doing it.

They were both a bit subdued when they came out, but the burger joint beefed up their spirits again, and before long, laden with plastic bags and paint cans, they were hitching their wet way home.

The third car that passed them pulled in. It was Jean. The back seat was down and the whole car was crammed full of feed bags. Annie spread-eagled herself on top of them and Michael squashed himself into the passenger floor space.

'My God,' said Jean, catching sight of his earring. 'Whatever she's got, it's contagious.'

* * *

After they'd unloaded the feed, Jean orchestrated a major rearrangement in the yard. The biggest horses were moved into the four new boxes, and several newcomers and youngsters that Jean wanted to get working on were brought in from the fields. Somehow or other the numbers didn't add up, and Bandit had to be turned out in a New Zealand rug. Annie was disgusted.

'He'll catch his death!' she whined.

'That'll be the day,' said Jean.

They swept all the dragged straw and hoof emptyings up off the yard, then Michael took Horrocks out for a school over the jumps, and Annie got roped in to hold the sport horse while Jean gave him a trace clip. She was full of herself afterwards.

'He didn't like it at all, but I hung on to him, didn't I, Jean? I didn't let him get away.'

'You might get that flat in the horsebox yet,' said Michael. 'You might even get it rent-free.'

But it was the wrong thing to say. Annie's mood deflated, and he hovered helplessly, too tall again all of a sudden; too gangly to know where his feet were.

He took her down to the closed-up gate. Together they cleared away the reaching brambles and the brittle, brown remains of last year's weeds. Beneath them Michael could see new growth beginning; the shoots pale and vulnerable against the brown earth. He was glad to see them. The leaves would soon follow, and the grass in the tired meadows. The horses would begin to fatten and shine.

He let Annie continue with the clearing while he set to work with the wire cutters. But even when they had removed all the entanglements, they couldn't get the gate open. The ground had closed over the bottom bar and they had to go back and get spades to dig it out.

By the time they were finished, it was almost dark. As they walked back to the house, the spades over their shoulders, Michael plucked up courage.

'If you ever wanted to talk about it . . .' he said.

'About what?'

'I don't know. Your mum and everything.'

Annie shrugged. 'Nothing to talk about, really. She's got MS. Had it about four years.'

'Do you mind?' said Michael. 'I mean, helping her and all that.'

'What's the point in minding?' said Annie. 'You do what you have to do, don't you?'

There was a small silence, then Michael said, 'And what about your dad?'

He sensed her immediate withdrawal from him. 'What about him?'

'I don't know. Just . . . If you ever wanted to talk about it . . .'

'I'll let you know,' she said coldly.

Back in the yard, Frank was getting out of the lorry. Amazingly, it wasn't rattling or rocking about on its springs. It was empty.

The four of them gathered around the fire with glasses of Baileys and ice, and drank a toast to Frank's long-awaited acquisition of sense.

After dinner they sat around the kitchen table, composing the next set of advertisements for the papers. They started with the grey mare. No one could remember how many points she had won, and Michael couldn't be bothered to go hunting through the records.

'Just put: "Will take the right rider to the top."'

'A competent rider,' said Frank.

'Perfect,' said Jean, writing it down.

They wrote a spiel for Horrocks, and one for The Menace, who was pretty much sound again. Then they got round to Bandit.

It was a minute or two before Annie realized who the chestnut cob was that they were discussing. When she did, she was appalled.

'Bandit?' she gasped. 'You can't sell Bandit!'

'We know that,' said Frank. 'But we live in hope.'

Michael's tattoo stung like hell when he went to bed, but he was well accustomed to living with aches and pains, and it wasn't that that kept him awake. It was Annie, beneath his roof, just a wall away.

How could she be so close one minute and so distant the next? How could she plunge so fast into the dark; into the secret horror-chambers of her heart? He could help her if she let him; he was somehow certain of that. He could break those doors down, beat off the ravens, haul out the tyrant by his blue beard and strike off his head. But she had to give him the chance. She had to show him the way.

He saw her arm again, bared in the tattoo parlour. All those lines were a code he could not crack; the hieroglyphic record of her past; the cardiogram of her damaged heart. He turned over and, filling him with a sudden, cold dread, the river was singing its black, oily music.

. . . wondrous deep . . . wondrous bonny . . .

How long was it since a voice first gave birth to those words? A hundred years? Two hundred? When did Annie's old willow fall? When did the bushes blacken and shrivel? How long had that stretch of the bank been bare?

. . . never more I'll see my Annie . . .

My Annie. He didn't slam his head into the pillow. The words were no longer taboo. They were the incubators of his newborn hopes. They were the hearth fires of his dreams.

Annie, wearing her helmet, was already in the kitchen when Michael came down in the morning. He edged around her as she made the tea, afraid of the touch he longed for.

The rain was falling heavily. When Jean got up she looked out of the window and shook her head. It only happened about twice a year that they didn't ride out, and usually it was as a result of a hard, hard frost which left the roads like glass and the fields as solid as concrete. Michael looked out again and understood. It was sheeting down out there. It was the kind of rain that drenched you as you made a dash for the car; that made roads into streams; that swept the stableyard for you and left the sweepings in neat piles around the edges of the drains.

Jean poured two cups of tea and returned upstairs. Michael poured two more. He and Annie sat at the kitchen table to drink them.

'It's my fault,' said Annie. 'I'm bad luck.'

'Where did you get that idea?'

She shrugged. 'It's the same wherever I go.'

'Well, you're not bad luck here,' said Michael. 'It's good luck for me to get a morning off.'

'But you can't ride!'

'Oh, Annie.' He wanted to hold her. 'Riding's just a job for us. Every morning, day in, day out. We're all sick to death of it.'

The idea was incomprehensible to Annie. 'Well,' she said, 'I'm going to get Bandit, anyway.'

'Wait for a bit. It might ease off.'

She shook her head. 'He's all wet and cold. I want to see him.'

There was no arguing with her. He found slickers and leggings for them both and they waded down to the paddock beside the green lane. Bandit was standing in the corner with the other horses. The tree they were under gave them no shelter from the rain at all, but as Michael drew near to it he noticed that it was coming into bud.

'See?' he said to Annie. 'The spring's almost here.'

'New life,' said Annie. 'New hope.'

Bandit whickered gruffly through his nose as they approached through the ink and water dawn. Michael took Annie's hand and guided it between the rug and the horse's shoulder. It was warm and dry in there.

Annie smiled, conceding his point, but she left her hand where it was, beneath his, for a moment; two moments more.

'We might as well go out,' said Michael, as they tied Bandit to the pillar of the hay shed. 'We're hardly going to get any wetter.'

'Yess!' said Annie.

Michael watched from the grey mare's box as Annie attempted to tack up the cob. No other horse in the yard would have put up with her. She took his head collar off first, and left him standing free while she tried to make sense of the bridle. Then she put it over his ears, leaving the bit dangling on his nose. On the next attempt she held the bit in both hands and offered it to him as though it was some special kind of treat. The big, kind oaf of a horse took it, but Annie still couldn't figure out where the other parts went. The bridle was facing backwards. She pulled the nose-band over his ears and was trying to thread the throatlatch through it when Michael decided it was time to intervene.

He showed her how it was done. She took it off and put it on again three more times. Bandit didn't move a muscle, except to let out a colossal, exasperated sigh.

They rode through the newly opened gate and along the green track, splashing through puddles and pools, dislodging the gathered rain from the leaning branches to stream down their waterproofs. Tiny waterfalls ran off the hems of their leggings and the toes of their boots.

They trotted a lot, cantered a bit, Bandit's great saucepan feet throwing up muddy geysers all around him. By the time they came back, the rain had abruptly stopped and the sun was breaking through. The water lying everywhere across the land mirrored its light. The whole world shone like gold.

While Annie took Bandit back to the field, Michael went in to put the breakfast on. Jean was sitting at a table with a calculator and a cheque book, sorting the paper stack into orderly piles.

'You never showed me this,' she said.

Michael glanced at the crumpled letter on the school's headed paper.

'I did.'

'Michael. You didn't. You didn't show it to Frank, either.'

'What's it doing there, then?'

Jean sighed and walked up behind him. He was dropping sausages into the fat melting in the pan. She put a hand on his shoulder, above the secret tattoo.

'Is anything bothering you? At school, I mean?'

The hand felt like a claw; a vice; an alien thing.

Beneath it, the caduceus burned his flesh.

'Frank says they're worried about you.'

A gasket blew in Michael's head. He elbowed Jean's arm aside and turned to face her. He was a full head taller.

'What the hell does it matter?' he stormed. 'Nobody gives a toss about me. Nobody ever has!'

'That's not true, Michael!'

But he was already halfway up the stairs, and her words ran off him like the rain.

He had already started painting when Annie came up with their breakfasts.

'Your mum said you had a row.'

'Not really,' said Michael. 'She just got up my nose, that's all.'

'They do,' said Annie.

When they'd eaten they carried on painting: two boards white; every third one black. The gloss didn't cover well; the old colour showed through, like the nicotine stains on a smoker's fingers.

'It doesn't matter,' said Annie. 'We can go over it again.'

'And again,' said Michael.

'Andagainandagainandagain,' said Annie. She was back to her bubbly best. For Michael, nothing else mattered.

They carried on painting until the fumes built up in

the airless space and began to make them nauseous. The sun had gone in, but it wasn't raining again. Not quite.

Jean was just coming into the yard with a filly on the lunge line.

'Do me a favour, Michael?' she said. 'There's someone coming to look at that skewbald mare in the morning, and she hasn't been out of her box for a week. Throw my tack on her, will you, while I grab a coffee?'

It was her way, obtuse as it was, of making amends. Normalizing relations.

Michael accepted the gesture. 'No problem.'

'Can I brush her?' said Annie.

They all met up again in the dairy; Jean returning the lunging cavesson, Michael and Annie gathering tack.

'Put studs in her, will you?' said Jean. 'It's like a skating rink out there with all this rain.'

The brown and white mare was round the back of the yard, in what had once been a fuel shed. Frank hadn't got round to putting a half door in yet, and the only light came from a small, cobwebby window.

Annie was slow with the brushes. She didn't really know what she was doing, and Michael didn't like to keep correcting her. She had her own style in everything she did. He sat in the manger, sifting hayseeds, while she worked.

When she had been all over the mare with the body brush, she picked a metal curry comb out of the box.

'What's this for?'

'Cleaning the brush.'

He went over to show her; scraped the dusty brush across the comb's sharp teeth. She nodded, rolled up her sleeves and reached for them back, but Michael put them down and took her hands instead.

She didn't pull away. He ran his fingers over her scarred forearm. She watched. Then he kissed her.

They were still kissing, utterly lost in the sensations of their bodies, when Jean called from the yard. They broke apart quickly. Adrenalin mixed with the other hormones already storming Michael's brain. He flung the tack on the mare and, fixing a dutiful mask on his face, led her out. Annie followed with the grooming kit.

Michael gave his mother a leg-up. She reached under her saddle flap to tighten the girth.

'You might come down in a few minutes,' she said. 'Give us a hand with the jumps.' She paused. 'Is there nothing you should be schooling yourself?'

'I'm giving them a Sunday,' said Michael. He was glad they'd already had a row. It meant they couldn't have another.

The minute Jean disappeared round the end of the block, Michael turned back to Annie. She grinned, led him back into the dark shed, leaned back against the lime-washed wall beside the door. They kissed again. Michael tasted the metal stud in her tongue. Her fingers on his back sent tremors through his skin. He pressed his body against hers.

'Ow!'

She pushed him away and probed in his shirt pocket. Small, heavy pieces of metal moved in there.

'What's this?' She was holding up a tiny spanner.

'Oh, no,' said Michael.

The studs for the mare's shoes. He had forgotten to put them in.

He ran through the yard, Annie close at his heels. It was sure to be all right. Jean wouldn't be asking the mare any serious questions yet.

She wasn't. They were down at the narrow end of the flat paddock, away from the jumps, just moving up into a canter.

Michael called. Jean looked up but didn't stop. He ran on and arrived at the fence just as Jean pushed the mare into her bridle and turned her into a tighter circle. Michael called out again, but it was already too late. The mare's legs went out from under her and she crashed to the ground.

Jean was thrown clear. She landed on her left shoulder and flipped over onto her back. The mare scrambled to her feet and shook herself, making the saddle flaps rattle. Jean should have been up too. Michael had seen worse falls; plenty of them. But she lay there a bit too long before she moved. As he helped her sit up, her face was as white as the sky.

'I'm sorry, Mum. I forgot the studs. I was just coming down with them.'

Jean's jaw was set against the pain. She was already clutching her left wrist in a familiar way, up against her right cheek.

Annie crouched down beside them. 'Are you all right?'

Jean shook her head, clamped her good elbow over Michael's offered arm and let out a string of profanities as he helped her to her feet.

'My flaming collarbone again,' she raged. 'That's the fifth time!'

Annie caught the mare and ran on ahead with her to the yard. By the time Michael and Jean had struggled up to the house, she had a fire lit and the kettle on.

'I'll ring Dad on the mobile,' said Michael. 'Where is he?'

'Yorkshire,' said Jean. 'Tying up loose ends.'

'Oh, great,' said Michael. Jimmy was away as well. There was no one else they knew.

'We'll have to go in the box,' said Jean.

'I'll drive, then,' said Michael.

He had driven the box loads of times in the yard and

the fields, and down the long avenue that led to their farm in Yorkshire. He was sure that he was up to it.

'Don't be ridiculous,' said Jean. 'I'm perfectly capable of driving. But I'll have to get out of this mud, first.'

Michael waited in the kitchen while Annie helped Jean change her clothes. She was used to it, he supposed, after tending to the needs of her own mother. His heart swelled with guilty pride. His girl, his Annie, here in the house, practically part of the family. Helper of mothers, clearer of chimneys, kindler of long-dormant fires.

My Annie.

Michael made a sling for Jean out of a green tail bandage and a red headscarf. It made her arm look like some kind of sick Christmas joke. He sat up beside her and changed gear for her as she drove. Annie sat beside the window, the dogs at her feet.

It was a bit hairy at times. The movement of Jean's good arm on the huge steering wheel clearly aggravated the collarbone, and there were times when her face was so pale that Michael feared she'd pass out. Sometimes she forgot to tell him to change gear, and once he dropped it into second instead of fourth and nearly had them all out through the windscreen. But they made it eventually, and pulled up outside the casualty department.

While Jean registered, Annie ran off and came back with the cup of tea that they hadn't waited to make at home. She fitted in so well in everything they did. It made Michael realize something; one of the reasons their lives were so stretched and colourless. There just weren't enough of them. Not since Fiona left and Joanne died.

A man in a starched uniform shirt approached them. 'Is that your lorry outside?'

It wasn't a difficult call, given the mud and the wellies.

'You'll have to move it. It's in the way of the ambulances.'

Jean got wretchedly to her feet, but Michael pressed her down again.

'I'll shift it, Mum. Give us the keys.'

The skies had opened again. The gutters outside casualty were swift waterways. Cigarette butts bobbed on their currents.

Michael made a dash for the lorry, hauled himself up over the wheel arch, shook the heavy drops from his hair. The engine started instantly and idled, as it always did, in great, heaving shudders.

The sky was dark and the wing mirrors were rain spattered. Michael opened the window and craned his head through before easing out on to the empty road. The hospital car park looked full. In any case, it wasn't designed for a six-horse box, the height and width of a bus. He turned in the other direction, past a confusion of arrowed signs, pointing to different wings and departments. All the roads had fresh double-yellow lines.

Just as he passed a left turn which led towards the maternity unit, he saw his chance. A trampled lawn ran up to the edge of the road. If he reversed tightly, he could park the left-hand wheels on the grass and leave the right-hand ones on the edge of the road. It might not meet with much approval, but he wouldn't be obstructing anybody.

The passenger side wing mirror was doubly obscured, by rain on its surface and on the window. But Michael had already seen that the road was clear. The main thing was to act quickly, before anything came up behind him.

The gearbox grated as he engaged reverse. The clutch, as always, was short on travel. Despite his careful precautions, the lorry went backwards in a series of ungainly lurches. Michael stopped to get his bearings and found that he was sweating. His hands left damp patches on the steering wheel. He leaned over to look out of the opposite window. The front wheels were still out in the middle of the road, but he appeared to have got his angle right. All he had to do was to reverse another few metres.

There was nothing to be seen in the wing mirror. He found reverse again and let out the clutch.

He heard the blare of the horn and his foot hit the brake, but the crash had already happened. Rigid with terror, Michael pulled on the handbrake and got out of the cab. The driver of the car was already beside it, staring at the crumpled wing and bonnet of her smart hatchback.

'What the hell did you think you were doing?' she said.

'You must have come up behind me,' said Michael. 'There's a blind spot in all them lorries.'

She stared at the horsebox as if it had just dropped out of the sky. 'What's it doing here, anyway?'

Michael looked at it as well. There wasn't a mark on it.

She could have been a lot harder on him. When he told her his mother was in casualty she seemed appreciative that neither of them had ended up there as well, and agreed that there was no need to involve the police. Instead, she called over a passing technician to act as a witness while she wrote down the registration number and took the insurance details from a grubby document that Michael found in the glove box. When she asked him for his name, Michael gave her Frank's. Just in case.

He was shaking when he got back into the building. Annie was waiting for him. Jean had been seen by a doctor and had gone on to wait her turn at the X-ray department.

Michael told Annie about the accident.

'You didn't admit it, did you?' she said. 'You didn't agree it was your fault?'

'Well . . .'

'You should never do that. You should've said she drove into you.'

'But she didn't.'

'You still should have said it.'

'It doesn't matter. As long as she keeps the cops off my back.'

'I suppose,' said Annie.

'Promise you won't tell my mum?'

'She's going to find out soon enough, isn't she?'

'Soon enough will do,' said Michael. 'Promise?'

Jean was still waiting for her X-ray. She knew the procedure backwards by now.

'The doctors here haven't seen my famous collarbone before,' she said. 'There'll be all sorts of palaver when they see those prints.'

'Shall we get you something to eat?' said Annie.

Jean shook her head. 'I couldn't stomach anything now. You go off, though. Come back in an hour.'

'You sure?' said Michael.

'Positive.'

They walked out for a takeaway and ate it in the lorry while the dogs went out for a run. When they'd finished, Annie climbed up into the transom and

Michael squeezed in beside her. They lay in each other's arms, listening to the downpour on the roof while the day faded away and abandoned them to darkness.

'I hate this,' Michael found himself saying.

'What?' said Annie.

'All this. Hospitals. Accidents. I've had enough of it.'

'Your mum's collarbone?'

'Not just that.' He told her, then, about Joanne. He hadn't intended to. It wasn't something that he ever talked about. But now it spilled out; the whole story in all its tragic detail.

Annie said nothing until he had finished speaking. Then she held him tighter and rubbed his shoulder. 'Oh, Michael.'

She was too close now to shut him out again. He ran his hand over her arm; felt the scars like hard worms under her skin.

'Why do you do it?'

'I don't know,' she said. 'I just get this pressure inside. It builds up and up. The only way to get rid of it is to cut myself.'

'Why?'

'I told you. I don't know.'

He was afraid to pursue it, but he had to. 'Is it something to do with your dad?'

She wriggled as if she was uncomfortable. 'Maybe it is.'

'How long has he been inside?'

'Three years.'

'Do you ever visit him?'

'I went once. He blubbed like a baby. I never went again.'

'What did he do to you, Annie?'

She didn't answer, and he was afraid that he'd been wrong; that she'd frozen him out again.

'I'm sorry,' he said.

But she shook her head and a hot tear dropped onto his neck. He held her tighter.

'Come on, Annie. You can come and live with us, you know. My mum and dad are mad about you.'

The sound she made could have been a laugh or a sob. 'It's too close,' she said. 'I have to get further away than that.'

The wind played the rain like a snare drum above their heads. Michael listened to it, and the fluty sound of the trickling scuppers.

Never more . . .

'I'm coming with you if you go,' he said.

He changed the gears again on the way home. Jean regaled them with stories of X-rays and horrified doctors, but Michael's gaze was fixed on the wet road. Dead leaves scudded across it like injured mice. The slanting rain was a subtle mesh, fencing him in. Tree trunks and telegraph poles slid in and out of the lorry lights; each one a milestone on a road of no return.

Leading him towards the Annan Water.

The van was waiting in the yard. Jimmy got out and helped Jean out of the lorry.

'Are you all right?'

'I'm fine,' she said. 'Just a little fracture. We weren't expecting you until tomorrow.'

Jimmy looked acutely unhappy. 'It didn't take as long as we expected. Ruth is going to need to talk to Annie.'

Michael went with her to gather her things.

'Ring me,' he said. 'Come tomorrow if you can.'

She nodded, but he could see that she was distressed.

'*Ruth is going to need to talk to Annie*,' she said. 'What do you think that means?'

'I don't know.'

'I do.'

'What?'

She took the flimsy carrier from his hand. 'If we're going to get our act together it had better be soon.'

She was gone, out across the wet and whickering yard and into the van. Michael stood in the kitchen, listening to the engine fading out along the road.

In the sitting room, Jean said, 'Damn!'

'What is it?' he asked.

'Oh, it's nothing,' said Jean, but there was a catch in her throat; she was close to the end of her endurance. 'It's just that the fire's gone out.'

In the sodden, squelching darkness he carried a bale of hay down to the horses in the field. They crowded around him, snatching wisps from the bale. He broke it, tossed the fragrant flakes in different directions, and they split off in pursuit.

He shone the torch on them, one at a time. Bandit's rug had slipped. Michael straightened it, then leaned for a while against the cob's flat withers, watching him tear at the hay.

'You like Annie, don't you?' he said to him quietly. 'So do I.'

With Frank away and Jean done up, Michael had everyone's work to do that night. All the injections to be given, the haynets to fill, the water buckets sloshing into his wellies. After that there were feeds to be measured and mixed, beet pulp to be soaked, dogs to be found and fed.

Jean, long practised in the art, had made a one-handed meal of scrambled eggs on toast. Michael swallowed it down, even though there seemed to be nowhere for it to go. His whole body felt as if it was full of some toxic, leaden compound that slowed down his movements and made him feel cold. He filled a hot-water bottle for Jean, then took himself up to bed.

But his room was still stinking with fumes. The streaky, half-painted walls disturbed his brain patterns. The floor was a litter of newspapers, paint tins, jars of black and white turps. He went into Annie's room instead and got into the bed. The sheets still held a faint trace of her sweetness.

I loathe that she should wet her feet
Because I love her more than any.

What had she meant? What was her mother going to talk to her about?

The sides are steep, the water's deep,
From bank to brae the water's pouring . . .

'If we're going to get our act together . . .'
What did she mean by that? Was she really going to

leave home? And if she did, was he really going to go with her?

In the early hours of the morning he woke to the sound of a car pulling into the yard. For a few moments of wild joy he held his breath, certain that it was Jimmy, bringing Annie back to him. But it was Frank's tread in the yard, Frank's key in the lock, Frank's quiet voice calming down the excited dogs.

Frank hit the roof when he saw the state of Michael's room. His indignation boomed throughout the house.

'What is this place? A madhouse?'

Jean must have answered. Michael couldn't hear her.

'But he's painting pedestrian crossings on his walls!'

Jean answered again. Michael heard her voice but not her words. She was still in her bedroom across the hall; maybe still in bed.

'I know, I know,' Frank said impatiently. And then, more acquiescently, 'I know.'

It was broad daylight. The traffic noise was already loud and persistent. There would be no roadwork again that day.

There was no show either. It would have been a great day to give Annie a lesson. Michael thought of phoning her, but she still hadn't given him her number. He didn't even know what her surname was. That was crazy.

They'd barely finished breakfast when the girl who was interested in the grey mare turned up, un-announced, with her father. It was a canny trick, designed to stop sellers 'preparing' a horse for a prospective customer; doping a lame one, perhaps, or riding a dangerous one into the ground.

'Sit down and have a cup of tea,' said Jean.

They did, but it was clear that they were uneasy in the cold, lean kitchen.

Michael wished he'd had warning. He would at least have moved the pony into one of the new stables. It cheapened her somehow, to be seen in a narrow cattle stall, no matter what explanations he might give. What was worse, he hadn't mucked her out for two days. Her hocks and knees were covered in yellow-brown stains.

But the rest of her coat was clean beneath her rug when he pulled it off her in the yard.

'Sound in every way,' said Frank. 'Open to any vet you like.'

The man nodded and circled the pony. There was no way he could fault her conformation. She had none of the narrowness that sometimes spoiled pony breeds as they grew closer to the thoroughbred look that show judges tended to favour. She was a round-barrelled, powerful little tank of a pony. She was a bonny grey mare.

Michael let the girl brush her over, pick out her feet, tack her up. He put the studs in himself, though, to be sure they were tight. They couldn't afford any more mistakes.

He rode her first; put her through her paces in his usual professional way. When he was satisfied that she was as settled as she was likely to get, he jumped down and gave the girl a leg-up. Of all the riders who had sat up on that pony, the girl got on with her the best. She was the right kind of rider for her: light-handed and fearless. Even when the mare fizzed and fretted, the girl didn't panic, but relaxed; wound her down; did all the right things.

Her father and Frank were leaning against the paddock rail. Michael heard nothing of their conversation until the girl had done as much as she wanted and they returned to the gate.

'I tell you,' Frank was saying, 'if you're still fixed on this trial business you're wasting my time as well as your own.'

There was an awkward silence, during which it became clear that the man was, indeed, still set on the trial.

Frank sighed. 'Listen,' he said. 'Do me a favour, will you?'

Michael stiffened. Frank often followed that question with dreadful, insulting suggestions. But this time he was being constructive.

'Have a look at our chestnut pony. Have a go on him. If you don't like him, you don't like him. If you do, you can take him away for a week. Take him to a show. Take him to the pony club. Take him up Mount Everest if you like. But this lady isn't leaving my yard till I have cash in my hand.'

The girl rode back to the yard. As Michael untacked the mare and put her rug back on, she said, 'She's beautiful. You must be mad about her.'

For an instant, Michael thought she was talking about Annie. Then he realized. 'I am,' he said automatically. But he found himself looking at the pony again, through Annie's fresh, appreciative eyes.

'I really am,' he said, and meant it. 'I'll miss her when she goes.'

The chestnut was younger and a lot less experienced than the grey, but much steadier. He too responded well to the girl's sympathetic style. She took her time to get him balanced, then jumped him round a small course.

'You don't have to start at the top, you know,' Frank said to her father. 'There's a lot to be said for bringing a good pony up through the grades.'

Then, to Michael's surprise, he went into the paddock and put up an enormous spread. It was bigger than anything the pony had faced before.

'Away you go.'

It was a gamble. The pony would have been justified in refusing. But he spotted the fence early, sorted himself out well and sailed over it. As he returned to the watchers at the gate, there was a spark of pride in his brown eye.

The girl was thrilled to bits; a huge, beaming grin in a riding hat. She patted the pony over and over again.

Frank could judge them, all right. Not just ponies either, but people as well.

They delivered the chestnut straight away. The girl went with them in the lorry to show them the way. The smile never once left her face.

Her father had gone on ahead and prepared their smart wooden loosebox for the visitor. The pony rolled in the deep straw, making himself at home. As they walked away and left him, Michael came to a realization, but it wasn't until he was back in the horse-box heading home that the full significance of it dawned upon him.

He always had a handful of ponies in his string: two or three on the show circuit, another couple of young or green ones coming on behind. But if this one, as seemed likely, didn't come back to them, he would be left with only one.

Frank and Jean weren't buying him any more ponies. The grey mare was the last one. When she was gone, there would only be horses. He would be an adult rider, making his way in the adult world.

'Did anyone phone?' said Michael.

Jean shook her head. She was going through the paper stack again, more thoroughly this time. There was a litter of old magazines and screwed-up letters on the floor beside her.

Michael gathered them up and dumped them in the sitting room, beside the sooty sticks. The fire was unlit, but the room still smelled of woodsmoke. He wished he had a mobile. He'd been given one for his birthday the previous year, but it had fallen out of his pocket into a bucket of water a few days later. He ought to have got one on Thursday. He ought to have got one for Annie as well. He had the money.

Next time. Soon.

A dreadful anxiety gnawed at him perpetually. Several times during the day he thought about going to see her. He dreamed of turning up at Jimmy's house with Bandit and asking him to fetch her; of cycling down and going across in the boat; of asking Frank to take him in the car, the long way, over the bridge.

But the day got swallowed up by horses, as every day before it and, foreseeably, every day beyond it. There was even more riding for him, now that Jean was grounded. There was even talk of him riding The Menace in the Open the next day, but he didn't get on well enough with him in the field. His stride was too long and Michael couldn't judge it. He was having to stand off his fences, or fiddle his way out of the bottom of them. At home it didn't matter. Faced with a big track, it could be disastrous.

It started a major row. Frank had been warned off riding six years before, after a lunatic part-Arab had reared up and fallen over backwards on top of him, breaking his pelvis and three vertebrae, and rupturing his spleen. He didn't count the roadwork as riding, even though he'd been dragged off by a following horse on more than one occasion. The last time Jean was laid up, he had threatened to take over her string, and had brought her to tears. He did exactly the same thing this time.

'There's no point in going to the flaming show if we can't take the decent horses.'

'Don't go, then!' said Jean. 'What does one show matter?'

'It won't be one show, though, will it? How long are

you going to have your hand tied round your neck?'

The last time it happened, Joanne had screamed at him, 'Leave her alone! She can't help it!'

Perhaps Frank remembered. Perhaps he just collared his temper, as he always did, sooner or later. Either way, the wind went out of his sails. He shook his head, as if wondering where he was, then walked around behind Jean's chair and kissed the top of her head.

The people who were supposed to come and look at the skewbald mare didn't turn up. No one was surprised. It happened all the time. None of them made allowances for punters; they never sat around and waited for them to arrive, but carried on with whatever they were doing and trusted that if anyone came they would track them down.

Someone did come to look at Bandit, though. A couple. They rang first, then arrived half an hour later. They looked, as a lot of visitors did, like a pair of new Volvos that had taken a wrong turn and found themselves in a breaker's yard.

Michael brought Bandit up from the field and took off his rug. The couple looked at him. He looked at them. There was clearly no enthusiasm on either side.

'We were looking for something,' the woman said, 'with a bit less bone.'

It was a polite way of saying that Bandit was an elephant. Michael wished they could have seen him out hunting; clever as a cat over the banks and ditches, using his head as well as his heart. There wasn't a smarter horse, or a more obliging one, in the yard. He might have told them so; offered them a day's hunting on him, if he hadn't been Annie's horse.

Frank showed them Horrocks, the skewbald mare, Oliver and the young Irish lad. They found fault with everything. The truth was that it wasn't the horses that they didn't like. It was dealers.

After the row about the show, Michael assumed they wouldn't be going. He coaxed himself to sleep that night with the promise that he would see Annie the next day, one way or another. He woke with the prospect still glowing, but in seconds it was extinguished.

It was 6.30. Frank was knocking on the door.

'Get up! Big day today!'

She rang, though, while they were away. Jean told him as soon as he came in.

'What did she say?'

'Nothing. Just to tell you she phoned.'

'Did you get her number?'

'No.'

'Why not? Why not? You should have asked her for her number!'

'How was I to know?' said Jean. But she was

laughing at him, and so was Frank.

Michael wanted to be angry, but he didn't make it. She'd phoned. She still loved him. He no longer knew what he had been so worried about. Everything was sure to be all right.

She wasn't only in his mind at school the following day. His whole skin was full of her. She inhabited his flesh. He felt her rings and studs in his face, her scars on his forearms, the lightness and grace of her feminine limbs. Her expressions, her gestures emanated from him. He was her, staring in surprise at Mr Burns.

'The school counsellor's office,' he was saying. 'At eleven fifteen. You'll like her. She's easy to talk to.'

Michael nodded, just ordinary, grey Michael again; in more trouble. Mr Burns wrote down the name for him, and the time. Michael stared at the written words until he lost focus, and was gazing at Annie again.

He left the school at morning break and went into town. He bought the two mobiles first – Pay-As-You-Go – then hung around in cafés and arcades until the schools closed and it was time to hitch home.

Unusually, Frank and Jean were both sitting in the kitchen. Michael made for the stairs, but Frank called him back.

'We're in a lot of trouble,' he said.

'Oh?'

'Why didn't you tell us?'

'What?'

Frank exploded, leaping to his feet. 'The flaming car! The flaming hospital!'

The blood raced into Michael's head. How had he managed to forget it? 'Oh,' he said. 'That.'

'Oh,' said Frank, with cruel sarcasm. 'That. You gormless bugger.'

'It was only a little tip.'

'A little tip?' said Frank in the same tone. 'A little three-thousand-pound tip.'

'Three grand?' said Michael stupidly.

Frank moved away, turning his fury towards the wall. 'I don't know where your head is at, Michael. I'm getting seriously worried.'

'If you'd just told us,' said Jean. 'I mean, these things happen. What did you think we would say?'

It hadn't been that. He could have coped with Jean's anger. What he had feared, that evening at the hospital, was something far worse. That her tenacious hold on the all-rightness of everything would finally give. And that she would fall.

They spent their lives with their backs to that abyss, struggling against its gravitational pull. But it was always there: Joanne's colossal absence. It lay beside them on the main road every morning, beneath the juggernaut wheels. It gaped between the bright rails of the show jumps. It rocked Jimmy Souter's boat on its swell.

. . . the water's deep . . .

Michael's knees gave way. He slumped onto a stool.

'The insurance company rang me,' said Frank. 'If I'd known I could have admitted it. Said it was me driving. Claimed it was a tit for tat. All sorted. Instead I gave them an earful.'

'Can't you phone them back?' said Michael.

'I did, when I worked it out. But they'd already got back to the other crowd. They've got the police involved now.'

A fresh shower of rain broke into the silence.

'You weren't at school,' said Jean.

'I was!'

'Michael . . .'

He ran up the stairs and into his room. He tore the boxes out of his bag, the phones out of the boxes. Then he changed into his mud-stiff jeans and went out into the yard.

Three thousand. The chestnut pony would fetch –
what? Eighteen hundred perhaps? Bandit? Not
enough. Meat price at the sales. Horrocks, the Irish
lad. They'd sell something, make it up somehow.

But the police. The police.

He heard Frank's footsteps in the yard, and slipped
into the grey mare's box. In the darkness he heard
Frank call, then get into the car and drive away.

The box was a stinking quagmire. Michael went
back for a barrow and fork.

Woe betide you . . .

'It's me,' he remembered Annie saying. 'I'm bad
luck.'

Woe betide you . . .

He didn't go in for his dinner. Jean came out to talk
to him, but he froze her out. She went away again. He
worked until every last horse in the yard was comfortable; every poultice changed, every net and bucket
filled. He was in the feed shed, mixing the evening
feeds, when Frank came back, smelling of beer and
cigarettes. He wasn't drunk; he never got drunk. He
didn't seem much happier either.

Michael stepped back and allowed him to continue
with the mixing of the feeds. He handed the empty

buckets over and stacked them when they were filled.

'You'll have to face this, Michael,' said Frank. 'We'll come up with the money some way or other, but you'll have to talk to the police. You're not running away this time.'

'Who says I'm running away?'

Frank's hand caught him behind the ear, turning off his world for an instant, leaving him reeling. He had never been hit before. Never.

'Shape up, will you? It's all going in one ear and out the other! You're in all kinds of trouble; not just the bloody lorry!'

Michael stared at his father. His head was stinging, but not half as much as his heart. His face contorted; he kicked over the stacked buckets and ran out into the rain.

Jean stood up when he slammed into the house. He didn't leave his boots at the door.

'What happened?'

He brushed past her, heedless of her shoulder, and was at the bottom of the stairs when the phone rang. His first instinct was to ignore it, but he hesitated. Then he knew.

'Hello?'

'Michael?'

'Annie. It's you.' There was silence on the other end. 'Are you OK?'

Her voice was thin. 'He's coming home. Tomorrow.'

'Oh, no.'

'Michael?'

'I'm here. What are you going to do?'

'I can't get Jimmy. I can't get over.'

He looked at his watch. It was after eleven o'clock. His head was spinning. 'Annie,' he said. 'I got mobiles for us. One each.'

'That's nice, Michael. They're going to be a lot of use.'

He struggled to understand, knowing that he was missing something.

'I'll ring you some time,' she said. 'Whenever I can.'

'Wait a minute . . .' he stuttered. 'What's happening?' In the background he heard Ruth calling.

'I have to go,' said Annie. 'Bye, Michael.'

'Annie!'

The line was dead.

'Oh, shit. Shit!' He dialled 1471. The number was withheld.

Why had he gabbled on about mobiles? Why had his head worked so slowly?

She couldn't get over. She was going to leave without him.

Jean was at his shoulder. 'Who was that? What's going on?'

'Where's Dad?' said Michael.

He met him at the back door, on his way in.

'Will you give me a lift to Annie's?'

'You what?'

'Please, Dad. Please. It's urgent!'

Jean had followed him. 'Listen, Michael. We know you like this girl—'

'Please, Dad!'

'This is barmy,' said Frank. 'It has to stop. You've gone way over the top.'

He couldn't make them understand. How could he?

He ran back out through the rain. Someone had moved his bike. Where was it? Not far. It was flat again. The foot pump. He'd have to get the torch. Get the chain back on.

It would all take far too long. There had to be a better way.

There was.

The sound of the mare's feet on the cobbles was smothered by the hammering of the rain. Michael vaulted up and felt her tense beneath him; her reckless energy undiminished by the night. She danced sideways, rocking and plunging as they passed the waterlogged jumps field. When her feet touched the grass between the meadows she leaped forward into a canter, her ears stretched forwards, looking for the gate in the darkness. She saw it wasn't there and took hold like a little racehorse.

Michael battled with her, breaking all his own rules in the effort to control her. Brambles whipped his face. Whenever he ducked his head, the mare took advantage and rocketed forward. The wet reins slithered in his hands.

The rain seemed to be coming from all directions at

once, hitting his face like hailstones, hurting his eyes. The mare's eager feet clattered on puddles and stones. He was still fighting for control when he heard thunder behind him; a heavy, spine-chilling drumroll. Not thunder. Some awful, flapping, apocalyptic enormity, born of the wild wind. Michael dropped his head, looked back beneath his right arm. Something white was bearing down on him. He flinched with the shock before his mind recognized the pale shape. It was the broad blaze on Bandit's face.

He was at the mare's heels, trying to nudge up alongside her on the narrow track. His huge feet were invisible in the dark, but Michael could imagine them striking into the pony's fetlocks; bringing her down. He took a swipe at the cob's nose.

'Get out of here, you jug-head! Go home!'

He might as well have told the rain to stop falling. The big, lumbering fool of a horse must have enjoyed his little outings down the track. Nothing Michael did was going to stop him now.

Everything was suddenly beyond his control. The mare had got her head down and was eating up the ground like a hunted deer. Branches were catching at his face and his hair. He was in danger of losing an eye. Suddenly resigned, Michael dropped his head down beside the mare's neck. He was night-blind; she was not. He abandoned himself to her.

O'er moor and moss and many's the mire . . .

She flew on, leaning into the bends, stretching out along the straights, powering up the inclines and launching herself over their brows. She had never been allowed to run like this before. All the schooling, the restriction, the months and years of steady, steady, steady was flung from her now; kicked away behind her flying heels.

This was what she had been born for.

Rain and sweat mingled on her neck beside Michael's face. He hung on. His mind raced ahead of them.

. . . boatman, come, put off your boat . . .

Why couldn't Annie get Jimmy? Where was he?

Bandit was still at their heels, amazingly fast for a horse of his bulk. A mad vision flashed across Michael's sight. He and Annie, riding off on horseback.

But where? Where would they go? What golden plains lay out there beyond the Annan Water?

The mare was losing speed. She was jumping fit, but not race fit. The spring was gone from her stride. Michael could have pulled her up now with no bother at all, but he didn't. He dug his heels into her sides. She ran on.

164

No golden plains. No Las Vegas. There were cities spilling their homeless on to the streets. There were cold days and colder nights. There were prisons.

They crossed the little road junction at full tilt.

Sparks from the mare's hooves flew like fire . . .

But she was flagging. He kicked her on again and she responded, still game. They had to be nearly there.

It couldn't be so bleak. He could work. Any horse yard would give him a job if they saw him ride. And Annie; what could Annie do? Anything. Paint, decorate, become an interior designer. She would know what to do. She always did. They would be fine.

He was pushing the mare at every stride now. She was tired; pulling out all the stops. Without warning, her feet clattered out on to tarmac. She slowed and stopped.

She couldn't have ridden a furlong more,
Had a thousand whips been laid upon her.

Michael turned her head towards the river and they walked the few metres until it came into view. His heart sank. It was a different river. No longer dark and oily; swelled from all the recent rain, it was bulging into its banks; breaking white water where the jetty snagged its flank. The boat was above the landing level, leaning against its painter.

The mare stopped dead, stricken by the sight. The forgotten line returned at last, unbidden.

The bonny grey mare she sweats for fear,
She stands to hear the water roaring.

He was suddenly cold. Fury rose up in him against the stupid old song that kept intruding upon his thoughts, as though it had some right to be there; as though it could possibly have anything to do with what was happening in his life.

But it didn't leave him.

. . . never more I'll see my Annie . . .

He turned the pony's head and trotted her up to Jimmy's house. Bandit jogged alongside, blowing like a steam engine.

The van was there, parked in the yard. Michael jumped down and let go of the reins, but both horses followed him anyway, into the garden and up to the front door. There was a light on in one of the downstairs rooms but no one answered his knock. He went round to the back. The horses went with him, snatching at shrubs on their way.

Through the window, Michael saw Jimmy. He was slumped over the kitchen table amidst a litter of beer cans and whisky bottles. The back door was wide open.

'Jimmy!'

'Wha'?'

He didn't even open his eyes. Michael shook him.

'Jimmy! Get up! We have to go across!'

Jimmy groaned. Turned the other side of his face to the table.

'Jimmy!'

It was no use. There was no way that Jimmy was going to get up. Michael suddenly knew why, as well. He wasn't the only one who was on the point of losing someone he loved.

He glanced around the shabby kitchen. Did a boat have a key? How did you drive it?

He couldn't. Even if the river wasn't in full spate he couldn't get into the boat in the rain and the dark and try to work out how to sail it.

He stepped back out into the night. The horses were still waiting for him; he was their only point of reference in this mad midnight world. He took the mare's reins, led her out of the garden and down along the road towards the river again.

And he has tried to swim that stream,
And he swam on both strong and steady . . .

But he wouldn't. It proved to him that the song was just that. It had no power over him. It could go back

167

to his grandmother's grave. Nothing, not even his love for Annie, would induce him to try and swim. It was all over.

The mare tugged at the reins, afraid of the river; anxious to go back to her dry box and her haynet. Beside her, Bandit stood calmly, his flanks still heaving but his gaze quite steady and clear.

No. It was crazy.

The broad white blaze turned towards Michael.

No. Horses didn't think. Horses didn't make suggestions.

No way. No way. But despite himself, Michael was already pulling the tack off the mare.

Even on its last holes the bridle barely fitted the cob's huge head. The bit pulled up the corners of his mouth. The short browband pulled the headpiece over the base of his ears. The noseband wouldn't fasten at all. But he stood, as solid and patient as a tractor, while Michael pulled off the New Zealand rug. The wind grabbed it and the mare swung away from its sudden, flapping mass and trotted away down the road. Michael picked up the saddle then dropped it again. There was no way the girth would reach.

He jumped up bareback. At the edge of the river Bandit stopped, dropped his head, examined the frothing swell. Relief and frustration met halfway in Michael's heart. The cob had finally said no.

But he hadn't. Bandit lifted his head and walked into the river. The water was up to his knees, then his chest, then Michael felt the sudden weightlessness as the cob's feet lost contact with the river bed. He was swimming.

The water lifted Michael from his back and tried to sweep him downstream. He clung to Bandit's mane, already aware that they weren't going to make it; that Bandit, despite his powerful efforts, was being dragged downstream as well. He made a grab for the bridle, trying to turn the cob back, but Bandit was obeying a different set of imperatives. His eyes were fixed on the far bank, and he was swimming for his life.

The river snatched at Michael's clothes, pulling him down, trying to break his desperate grip on Bandit's mane. He was chilled to the bone, gasping for breath, and still the song invaded him.

But the river was wide and strength did fail,
And never more he'll see his Annie.

Bandit battled on against the current. They were approaching the bank, but way downstream of the landing stage. The sides were sheer. There was nowhere for a horse or a boy to climb out. The swell slammed them against the muddy wall. Michael could feel Bandit scrabbling with his forelegs for a foothold that wasn't there. In the darkness he could see the horse's honest eye, wide with the first fear he had ever known. But, strangely, his own fear seemed to have left him, along with all hope. Some sort of an end would come soon. They would both go down together.

The torrent dragged them away from the bank and they drifted for a few metres downstream before Bandit's frantic efforts brought them back in again. Above Michael's head, a network of thin, black roots broke out of the mud. How could there be roots when there were no trees?

Then he knew where he was. Up there on the bank was the old willow stump where Annie had sat that day. Those roots would be as dead and as brittle as the twigs that she had knocked out of his chimney. There was no way they would bear his weight.

But his instinct was stronger than his reason. He reached out.

Oh Annan Water's wondrous deep,
And my love Annie is wondrous bonny,
I loathe that she should wet her feet
Because I love her more than any.
Go saddle for me the bonny grey mare,
Go saddle her soon and make her ready,
For I must cross that stream tonight,
Or never more I'll see my Annie.

And woe betide you, Annan Water,
By night you are a gloomy river,
And over you I'll build a bridge,
That never more true love may sever.

And he has ridden o'er field and fen,
O'er moor and moss and many's the mire,
His spurs of steel were sore to bite,
Sparks from the mare's hooves flew like fire.

The mare flew on o'er moor and moss,
And when she reached the Annan Water,
She couldn't have ridden a furlong more,
Had a thousand whips been laid upon her.

And woe betide you, Annan Water,
By night you are a gloomy river,
And over you I'll build a bridge,
That never more true love may sever.

Oh, boatman, come, put off your boat,
Put off your boat for gold and money,
For I must cross that stream tonight
Or never more I'll see my lady.
The sides are steep, the water's deep,
From bank to brae the water's pouring,
And the bonny grey mare she sweats for fear,
She stands to hear the water roaring.

And woe betide you, Annan Water,
By night you are a gloomy river,
And over you I'll build a bridge,
That never more true love may sever.

And he has tried to swim that stream,
And he swam on both strong and steady,
But the river was wide and strength did fail,
And never more he'll see his Annie.

And woe betide the willow wan,
And woe betide the bush and briar,
For they broke beneath her true love's hand,
When strength did fail and limbs did tire.

And woe betide you, Annan Water,
By night you are a gloomy river,
And over you I'll build a bridge,
That never more true love may sever.

Jimmy was still asleep at the kitchen table when Ruth phoned him the next morning to tell him that Annie had disappeared. On his way to the jetty he found the saddle in the road, and the New Zealand rug tangled up in a barbed wire fence.

His head wouldn't function properly. He gathered up the saddle and rug and carried them back to his yard. Behind the hay shed, shivering in the wind, stood the grey mare. He phoned Jean and Frank.

They came straight down in the car, but it wasn't until they saw the state of the river that they understood how serious the situation was. They went back to Jimmy's house and phoned Ruth. She hadn't seen Michael. Frank began to shake. Jimmy, his head all too clear by now, called the police.

The officer he spoke to didn't appear to take the situation very seriously. Teenagers ran off all the time, he told Jimmy. The best plan was to wait for a while and see if they turned up. But a short time later he phoned Jimmy back. A report had come in, from a man whose grounds backed onto the river further downstream. A dead horse had been washed up against his boathouse.

For three days the emergency services dragged the river and searched the banks. No sign of Michael was found. Photographs were circulated among the police throughout the country, but no reports of either of the teenagers came in.

Hopes began to fade.

Fiona came home, drawn back into the family by another tragedy. Friends came up from Yorkshire to help with the horses. They moved around quietly, appalled by the bad luck that Jean and Frank seemed unable to leave behind them. All kinds of people emerged from Jean's distant past, and brought food, and sat through the long, sleepless nights, administering what small comfort they could. Most of them knew the old song. None of them mentioned it.

Jean spoke to Ruth from time to time. They both

found it helpful. Her husband, Andrew, was taking good care of her, she said. Jimmy still went across to the land he rented on the other side, but he didn't call on her. The boundary that existed between them now was a lot harder to cross than the river.

Jean and Frank spent hours beside it, trudging its muddy banks with Jimmy, peering into its swollen tide. It taunted them with glimpses of colour: rubbish towed along in its undercurrents; an old jacket snarled up on a beached branch. But it revealed nothing of its secrets. Their hopes and prayers had no influence upon it. Day after day it raced on with the same blind hunger for the sea.

There was talk, this time initiated by Fiona: of giving up the horses, or of sizing down, or of turning the yard over to liveries. But nothing happened. Nothing changed. The horses had to be fed and exercised. Everyone mucked in. The grey mare looked on, growing fat in her stall.

A fortnight later, Frank and Fiona returned from road-work to find Jean waiting for them at the side of the road.

'They're alive!' she shouted. She was waving a book and a pink envelope.

Frank jumped down. 'What?'

'Look!'

She showed him the card. '*Happy birthday, Mum. Love from Michael. And from Annie too.*'

Frank's horses wandered off towards the water-barrel under the tap, trailing their reins. Fiona was still mounted; craning over her father's shoulder. His hand trembled as he examined the card.

'When was it posted?'

The padded envelope was stuffed into Jean's sling. It was postmarked Dumfries, the previous day.

They phoned the police, who said they'd pass on the

news to Annie's parents and make some enquiries in Dumfries. Then they drove down to the river to tell Jimmy. He was thrilled, and gave Jean a big hug.

'I knew, though,' he said. 'I knew that boy of yours wasn't dead.'

'How?'

He pointed vaguely to the river bank, then shook his head. 'I'll have to take you across,' he said. 'You won't be able to see properly from here.'

The water level had fallen, but even so Jean's nerves were ragged by the time they reached the other side. Andrew's car was parked in Ruth's drive, but the house was silent and dark. They passed it at a distance and walked along the little bare path which ran along the bank.

'I've been noticing, you see.' Jimmy pointed to the grass at the water's edge. 'See?'

The others saw nothing.

'Those new shoots,' he said. 'Those are brambles, there. And that's going to be a briar rose.'

Jean and Frank looked at each other in bewilderment, then at Jimmy.

'The sure proof is over there,' he said, indicating along the path ahead of them. 'That old tree there was dead before I was even born. And look at it now.' He walked over to the blackened stump. Jean and Frank followed. The three of them stood looking down at it.

'Or maybe it was never dead,' said Jimmy. 'Maybe it was just waiting.'

From the edges of the willow stump, a dozen new shoots had sprung. Coursing with discovered life, the strong young limbs stretched up towards the sun.